# vul ul pine

## CURSE

# *vulpine* CURSE

by

katherine silva

STRANGE WILDS PRESS

Published by Strange Wilds Press
Print first edition: April 30th, 2025

Cover design and interior formatting by Katherine Silva
www.katherinesilvaauthor.com
Strange Wilds Press Logo by MartaLeo
www.katherinesilvaauthor.com/strange-wilds-press

# FOR THOSE WHO GRIEVE

# ARE YOU AFRAID TO

# TALK?

## LOSING YOURSELF IN A WORLD OF

## NUMBNESS?

## PAIN?

## DESPAIR?

# Join ELIXER and watch those fears melt away!

## CORNER OF RESINA AVE & CHERRY PARK ROAD

## SUNDOWN

There are sutures holding me together
that I don't want to pull out.

DENIAL

# MAL VERDUGO

$\mathbf{T}$HE KID SHOULD WALK AWAY. HE'S IN A CITY OF FOXES.

Mal Verdugo: a place of everlasting lights, of motion and inertia. Luck that turns to pain and back to luck with each flicker. Don't approach the car with the dangerous man sitting inside watching you. Don't pretend to swallow back the fear and put on a brave face. Don't. That's how this place gets its teeth in you.

He still does.

"Hey."

Hugh's arm rests on the windowsill, the heat of early night caressing the hairs on the back of his hand and blustering through the dingy cab of the Mercedes. A hint of red sun runs along the desert horizon and it paints passersby in violent shades as he watches them through the murky windshield.

He can't make eye contact. He should. But he won't. Not yet.

"Excuse me." More insistent. Not taking the hint. Not walking away.

He turns. "What?"

"Have you seen this girl?" A photo flutters between the young man's fingers.

Hugh squints to see it though he already knows what she looks like. Curly disheveled hair, a smile—no—a frown—no—a Mona Lisa smile. Freckles striping across her upper cheeks and nose. She's sixteen. Old enough to have known better than to come here.

"No," he answers, not meeting the boy's eyes.

The kid's hand drops to his side and he mutters a swear under his breath.

"Who is she?" Hugh asks. It's the first question anyone has requested because no one else has cared to find out more. Instead, they've shut their doors, turned away, told him to piss off.

Give the boy a lick of concern that someone is at least curious. Give him hope.

"My sister." His chest swells when he says it and almost immediately deflates. "My stupid sister."

Hugh doesn't comment, only stares. The stare asks questions that his mouth can't elucidate well, especially not now. He's afraid if he opens his mouth again, something he doesn't want will come out.

He's not alone after all.

There's someone sitting in the passenger seat next to him that no one else can see. The way they're looking at him—he knows they are—is enough for his throat to swell with longing, with agony.

*Don't look at me like that. Don't remind me of what I'm missing.*

# BEFORE

SEARCHING.

The early spring air had turned cold again, its claws burrowing beneath the threads of Hugh's cable sweater. Fear kept him from noticing the chill. Desperation pulled at his attention like a kite zigzagging in a turbulent wind. He cupped his hands around his mouth and called Amos's name a third time. Once again, nothing but the owls responded, nothing but the faint rustles of creatures scurrying away in the grass.

He'd wandered. It had happened a few times before but always within sight of the house. The last time, Hugh had found Amos on the edge of the woods watching the retreating light from the day. The only reason he'd noticed was because the patio door was left open and a cool wind had blown in to distract him from whatever he'd been doing.

This time, it was the front door. This time, Hugh had walked half-way up the drive before panic prickled at the lower half of his face, and he couldn't keep his breathing under control.

"Where is he?" Ella had asked. The crayon drawing of a deer drinking from a river was all but forgotten on the kitchen table as she followed his every movement with her gaze. He put her in the back seat of the car and cautiously meandered the old Pontiac up their long driveway toward the main road. Headlights illuminated the blue-gray darkness as the car crunched over their little patch of land.

"I'm sure he's fine," he told her. "He's just gone for a short walk to stretch his legs."

Their dirt road, wash-boarded and muddy from the rain, reached the paved street that led toward town. A glance left or right showed nothing but the empty stretch of asphalt narrowing like ribbon into the distance. Hugh tried to think of which way Amos would go and quickly realized he had no idea. He had no idea what Amos was thinking when he vanished like this.

He didn't have time to deliberate. *Pick a direction.*

And he started to. Until Ella's head poked up between the seats next to him along with her outstretched arm. "There he is!"

It was neither left nor right but straight ahead, up the footpath through the brambles toward the train tracks...

# MAL VERDUGO

"SHE'S ONLY STUPID BECAUSE SHE THOUGHT...she could make the pain go away."

The kid is talking again and it's music to Hugh's ears, enough to distract him from the car's other occupant. "She doesn't understand how things are now. She just wants our mom back like nothing ever happened."

His stomach flips. Ah. That's what this is about. Why is it such a surprise? Everyone in this new version of the world has lost someone after all. Families don't just pack up and blast off to Disneyland on vacation anymore. They hide. Or they trudge north toward the promise of water. Most of the lakes and rivers are as dry as the jerky being sold from the vendor across the way.

"She heard about this grief clinic from someone and hitched a ride out here. That was four days ago."

Mal Verdugo attracts all kinds of people. They vanish here. People used to come to this city to seek their fortunes, to find fame, to do things they never would have been allowed or could have done back where they'd come from for fear of being found out. What happens in Mal Verdugo, stays in Mal Verdugo. Now, who cares? No one has personas they have to maintain. Everyone is equal in how fucked they are.

And it's so much easier for the ones who want others to disappear to make it happen.

"Do you know how many people there are in this city?" Hugh asks.

"A fuck ton," the kid answers.

"Then you know you're looking for a needle in a hayfield."

"Don't you mean 'haystack?'"

"All these people…" Hugh peers through the windshield toward a group of men and women as they bustle across what was once a main drag through town. In a world gone by, he might have imagined they were from a wedding party off to try their luck at the casinos, or a family meeting up for dinner at one of the bougie hotels. They scurried, eyes scampering, raggedy clothes fluttering.

*Escape. Escape.*

*Hide. Hide.*

He turns back to the boy. "There's a lot of dangerous people in this city. She's by herself. You still think you're going to find her?"

The thing in the passenger seat shuffles ever so slightly.

The hairs on the back of Hugh's neck prickle.

*"I thought you didn't care."*

Hugh clenches his grip around the steering wheel. "I don't," he mutters before he remembers that his partner is silent for other's ears.

The kid head tilts back in defiance. "You don't know her. You don't know what she's had to survive."

Hugh clears his throat. "Survive until she came out here."

"No one can stay strong forever. Even our mom knew that."

"Grief is an ocean you can swim in your whole life and not find your way out. Even the people you thought might come to rescue you aren't prepared for its riptide."

The boy regards him with a side-eye. "This is starting to sound a little personal with all the anecdotes…"

"My point is that you should leave." Hugh now makes eye contact. The boy looks like he's fresh out of college judging by the logo on his sweatshirt. His expression was full of naivete, of thinking he understands life and its struggles. Maybe he was getting the hang of it until the Collapse. Until he was left behind to wither in the midst of one of the worst droughts in the history of human civilization.

"I'm not leaving her behind," the kid says, his voice gone gruff and low. Rebellious. Angry. Guilty.

*You stupid, stupid child,* Hugh thinks as his hand slides down to the gearshift in the console between him and the passenger seat.

A hand skims into view over his, the color of desiccated bone, of necrosis, of ashes.

*"If you do this, there's no going back."*

Hugh closes his eyes. If he stays, he'll need to follow-through. He knows he's being watched. If he leaves…he'll probably get a few miles before the curse lays him out flat. He'll be forced to crash the car or careen it off the road into the desert sand, to die a lonely death in that coffin of what was once considered a luxury vehicle. It would be buried in subsequent sand storms, his skin dried and body excavated of its remaining wet and it would all end…finally. Just like he wanted.

Death could be his salvation.

# MONTHS AGO

Asweetness carried in on the wind, one that Hugh tasted on the back of his tongue. A thought cried out from somewhere inside, buried like a bird beneath a cave-in, in hurried, jagged breaths before it was finally crushed: spring.

Spring used to mean growth. It meant a warmer sun, soil that crumbled through his fingers and smelled richly of earth. It meant rain in heavy, beautiful drops that plucked against his skin when he was caught out in it, that plinked musically against the stones on their patio, the chimes dangling from their porch. When there was a *they* and he wasn't alone.

No. He made himself alone. This desolation was his doing and no one else's.

He pinched the bridge of his nose, flicked the sleepers from his eyes that had formed and focused on the window before him. Across the street from the empty apartment building he crouched in, the silhouettes were like dancers performing through sheer curtains against a velvet blossom of lights. He'd been here since yesterday afternoon, since the heat burned a red mark over the back of his neck and pressed in on him from every angle. His shirt was sticky; his slacks sweated through. And, nine hours later, here he was in the bosom of midnight waiting for a sign.

Maybe this was it: the scent of spring. He could walk out of that junker of a building and into the urban sprawl, get lost in the streets, in the decay and the refuse before finding a place where plants grew, even if they didn't need much water to survive. He could live like that: a succulent. A cactus. Something thorny and stark that fed on the near endless light and heat…

Distantly, the sound of Amos's laugh caught him off guard. *"Oh, come on!"* he chuckled. *"You're making yourself out to be some kind of emotionless husk!"*

"Well, I am. Without you," he said.

*"No, I know you too well."* The voice was close; a breath in his ear that made him warm. *"There's nothing that could freeze that soft heart of yours. Not even liquid nitrogen could do the job."*

Hugh shook his head in the empty room. "You don't know."

Amos had nothing to say to that.

In the room across the street, one of the shadows lowered itself onto a bed while another brushed their hair across the room. Through the flickering curtains, flashes of skin revealed themselves—a thigh, an ankle, a stomach… All tanned and glistening against the lights.

He thought of Amos's skin and how it welcomed the sun, his Italian heritage soaking in the rays as they planted marigolds in their garden or walked the meandering path to the woods. He belonged in the sun.

Hugh burned no matter what. Always.

He inhaled sharply and focused his gaze across the street once again.

The person brushing their hair tucked the tool away into a dresser drawer and joined their companion in the bed. The lights went out: the sign he'd waited for.

Hugh abandoned his position by the window, knees quaking as he stood for the first time in hours. He collected his rucksack from the corner of the dingy room and swept through the dilapidated kitchen out the apartment door. Down the stairs, his footfalls echoed through the building's bones and out into the dark streets of Axy Gable. Once a tourist trap back when this ramble of earth resembled a coastline, the ocean had lapped against the breakwater and called out to travelers to wade in its salty froth. The rocks stood now in goliath majesty leading out to a barren lighthouse in the midst of a sandy sea.

He'd never been here before the drought. But he'd seen its reputation printed on old travel brochures, one of which stuck from the back pocket of his jeans. Even now it was a place for people to hide in, to try and ignore the giant blister this world had become.

He crossed the street and slipped inside the dark mouth of the building's entrance. The lock on the door was crude and with nothing but a hammer and a flathead screwdriver from his pack, he broke through. Noise wasn't a concern.

Nighttime brought out crowds who'd hidden from the daylight like cockroaches and none of them interfered with each other. Self-preservation was how you survived. No sticking ones neck out for strangers. No questioning the shrieks in the alleys or crying in the gutters. No one was safe. No one was worth dying for.

Hugh slipped in, the foyer's air like cool linen. The sounds of voices tinged with static ricocheted through-out the front hall. He crept to the stairs and took each tread on the balls of his feet. His hand was already poised, the words of his spell percolating over his tongue as he recited. A room at the top of the stairs beckoned, aglow in the flickering lightshow from the television. His steps confidently guided him into the doorway.

In the green haze of television-fluoresced light, Hugh hardly noticed a twitch from the man who lay in the bed before his words fell. Dark eyes rolled back into the man's head, choked-off coughs sputtered and blood flourished from every open cavity on his face. It ran down the grooves of his nose, the hollows in his cheeks to his chin like rivers. The act was over before anything could begin which is how Hugh always preferred it.

No fight. No struggle. No suffering.

Quick.

The woman in the bed scrambled from it, a patter of her feet against the floor the only noise. Her long golden hair spilled down over her neck to her chest as she scrabbled for the sheet and swaddled herself in it. She gawked at Hugh's shadow, the only part of him he would let her see.

"I wondered which one of you he'd send," she muttered. Wonder did nothing to conceal the fright in her voice.

Hugh nudged his head toward the dead man in the bed. "Did you even know his name?"

Shame colored her expression for barely a second. "He told me. But I don't remember."

"You were hoping for a shield, someone who might give you enough time to sneak away again?"

"It worked the first time, didn't it?" she said.

Hugh swallowed. Yes. It had. And he'd paid for it when Steele had found out about his failed attempt. "Where is it?" he asked.

"You know I don't have it."

"You're lying."

The woman bristled, even took a step toward him. "It's gone," she reiterated. "Used it all. Earned none of it back. How the hell was I supposed to with things as they are?"

She was telling the truth, but it didn't make any difference. Just because the world had fallen didn't mean that loans became forgiven.

"You find any goddamn way you can," Hugh answered. "Because you know what the alternative is."

"What's the point anymore?" She shook her head and let go of the sheet. It crumpled soundlessly to the floor. "What is there to live for?"

Hugh stared at the naked woman in front of him and clenched his jaw.

*So much.*

Unclenched it.

*Nothing.*

"You find something," he muttered.

He couldn't tell if the chuckle that escaped her was hopeless or witless. Whatever it was, the woman slumped into the chair next to the window and put a hand in front of her mouth to stifle what was left of it. "That's something. The executioner giving the victim a pep talk. Who the fuck do you think you are?"

Who? Hugh didn't know. He hadn't known for several years. The only thing he was sure of was the thing he used to be.

"You're right," he said after a moment. He struck out his hand, fingers going rigid at the same time as her body. From across the room, the snap and crackle of bones in her neck clicked. He heard the flesh of her lips parting and the last essence of her breath as it left her. She wilted against the chair, skin and muscle, fat and bone draped over the wood. "Best not to wax philosophical with the dead."

From his coat pocket, he drew out his phone, opened the camera and clicked a picture of the dead woman, then turned and took another of her dead lover. As slowly as the approaching dawn, he searched the room. He found nothing but jewelry, expensive clothing, perfumes, skin care… Thousands of dollars wasted on trivial fluff.

When he was sure there was nothing else, he made to leave and finally noticed what was on the television. A film from nearly a decade ago he immediately recognized. The actor on screen flashed his co-star leading-lady a charming smile, his blue eyes softening and told her he'd return soon.

From across the room, the dead woman's eyes watched the screen. Two swimming pools flickering against the light as if, she too, were waiting for him to come back so she could breathe once more.

Hugh glared at the screen. He hated that look. He'd seen it too many times in the last few years. Steele had been ever the actor, ever the commander of emotion on screen. Off of it? Feeling didn't exist, swallowed by indifference. And he demanded that same apathy of everyone that worked beneath him.

Hugh silently slipped back into the darkness, away from the eyes and the blueness of Steele's gaze and subsequently, started his journey back to their source.

# BEFORE

"STAY IN THE CAR."

The words were tight in Hugh's throat as he tried to unclick his seatbelt and realized he'd never put it on. He flung the car door wide open, engine still running, and staggered out.

Amos had stopped at the top of the hill and was gazing down the iron rails as if he were expecting something.

Hugh shouted Amos's name and the wind ate it.

He scrambled across the road, his legs feeling too slow, too awkward. He avoided a rock and climbed the trail up to the tracks. This time when he shouted, Amos heard him. His husband turned, not even in surprise, but in bemusement, his brows knitted together.

Hugh put his hands on his arm gingerly. "Amos, are you okay?"

It crashed down on his partner then: the awareness, the confusion bleaching into distress as he took in the railroad and the distance he'd travelled from the house. "I…I'm sorry," he sputtered. Hugh watched his body shiver as he became aware of the cold. "I don't know what happened."

Hugh pulled Amos close, wrapping his arms around him, kissing his forehead. "Let's go home, okay?"

The despondent whistle of a train moaned in the distance.

In the car, Ella asked the question Hugh feared she might: why did you go to the train tracks? He'd tried to explain to her that Amos got confused sometimes, that he might not know why he did some of the things he did. That he might lose things. He might forget things. She still asked. And he couldn't blame her. But it hurt to see the chagrin carved in Amos's face and the silence that followed.

"What shall we have for dinner?" Hugh asked her as he negotiated a U-Turn on the road. Distraction was the best tactic.

The car rocked gently as he navigated it over unavoidable potholes. "Spaghetti? Remember I picked up some of those—what do you call them?—" He snaps his fingers repeatedly. "—garlic knots from the store yesterday. We could have those."

Amos looked lost, gazing out his window.

In the rearview mirror, Ella appeared to give his words some thought. And then, "But why—"

"Tell you what?" He pulled into the driveway and idled. "Let's just head over to Secundo's and get a pizza. Then your father won't make fun of me for messing up the recipe to his special sauce and we don't have to do dishes!"

The false joy was manic, a headache thrumming in his temples. He watched his daughter's reaction turn from stubborn curiosity to thrilled in a split second.

"Pizza!" she squealed. "Can we get pineapple? Please, please, please!"

"Yes. Yes."

It worked. It bloody worked. No matter that he'd have to suffer through that fibrous sweet polyp on the pizza; it didn't matter.

Hugh turned the car around, rode up the driveway like a boat at sea again, turned onto the road to town… He hesitantly peered toward Amos.

The smile on his face was forced. Distant. Entirely unconvincing.

Hugh reached over and put a hand on his and after a moment, Amos reciprocated.

"What if we get it with anchovies? Would that taste good?" Amos said under his breath to Hugh, pretending that Ella couldn't hear.

"No!" she yelled. "Yuck!"

"Or maybe we could get it with olives? Those little black ones?" Hugh said back.

"You two are so gross!"

Laughter inflated in the cold space of the car. The rest of the vacuum was jammed by an obnoxious song on the radio that Hugh wouldn't remember hearing again until that day in the Mechanic's garage years later.

# "I WANT TO BE WITH YOU AGAIN."

These words were the scraps left of the thing Hugh used to be. A malleable thing guided by emotion on a pottery wheel.

"I want to be with you again." It was all he could think as he trekked across lonely highways, glimpsing scratches of daylight as they punctured through night's waning grip. He clenched his fists around the steering wheel of a stolen car and reminisced on tenderness. If he were to hold those he'd lost in his hands now—these hands—he'd surely break them. Tenderness was not made for people who were hasty, for people who wished not to feel anymore.

But he remembered it. He remembered tucking little hands beneath buoyant blue covers, the glow from a soft nightlight, the whoosh of a breeze caressing in over her bedroom through her window. Lullaby and goodnight and sweet dreams, marshmallow and wrapped in a haze he couldn't penetrate because a part of him desperately wished to experience it once more… If he made himself remember the minutiae, it would run him through.

Ella. His daughter's name sat brittle on his tongue. As soon as he let himself think it, he stuffed it down, down deep into the dark. Let it hide away with the night where it was safe, where the fierceness of day couldn't burn the memory of her from him.

Hugh drove until the engine sputtered and ran out of gas in the valley, as the sun crested over the distant hills. He abandoned it and walked and as he walked, he anticipated how he would scorch before he found refuge from the sun's fury.

The light was nearly upon him when something reminiscent of humanity appeared over the next hill. The gas station was lost in time, the white and yellow and orange painted walls on its outside resembling a candy corn left to wither beneath the desert sun. Did candy corn dry up? It was an amusing thought, one that he almost *hmphed* at before it cast off, fleeing on strong gusts.

He stepped into the dirt lot and inspected the derelict vehicles, the ones with their front hoods propped open, their black innards a twist of coiled hoses and pipes, windshields sand-blasted and tires dry-rotted. An old stereo's static buzzed from the open garage door nearby followed by the off-key whistling of someone who was barely listening, not even the matching tune.

Hugh remembered this song. Strange. He had never liked it but now, he welcomed its familiarity. He stepped up to the open door and looked around the cluttered shop before his sights fell on a mechanic crouched by the back wheel of an old Chevy truck. His shadow was enough to alert the man to his arrival and enough to make him take pause from his work. His meaty hand was wrapped around a socket wrench. Hugh noticed his grip tighten ever so slightly.

"Petrol," Hugh said. "My car broke down a few miles from here. That's all I need."

The Mechanic turned his head slightly in Hugh's direction, but not so much as to show his face. "That accent. What's a limey like you doing all the way out here?"

"Well, I didn't realize I'd time traveled back to the eighteen hundreds," Hugh mumbled.

The sneer that crossed this man's face reminded Hugh of foxes gathered around the corpse of some unfortunate animal: lips curled, eyes testing. They roamed in the dry land between abandoned homes and their eerie cries lingered on his mind.

"What should I do about this?" the Mechanic said, more to himself than to Hugh. "A man walks out of the desert asking for gas. It sounds ludicrous. And yet…" The man's eyes shifted to a door nearby.

In the dusky light of the one lamp inside, Hugh could see a slovenly-kept desk, mounted with stacks of papers, silver-colored bits—perhaps screws or bolts—a dusty computer screen and keyboard, old fast-food containers…

Before Hugh could say another word, the man marched into the office.

Alarm exploded from every pore in Hugh's body. He simultaneously gave chase and eyed places where he could duck if needed. Behind a gathering of oil drums seemed like the best cover but not if he could gather the energy needed for a spell…

Even as the thoughts gyrated, Hugh slowed his steps, his brain catching up with his eyes. There was no attempt to go for a hidden weapon, no hostility in the Mechanic's movements. Instead, he waggled the computer mouse around on its track pad and the monitor jolted to life, revealing a half-full page on a word document. The Mechanic diligently plucked at the keyboard and words strung into sentences.

Hugh's gaze narrowed. "What are you doing?"

The Mechanic put up a finger before returning to his typing. "You…" he said hesitantly, "…gave me an idea."

"For what?"

"My story."

Hugh's sights took flight around the office. Then the garage. Back to the rotting exterior of the shop where the sun had risen to its full height since he'd slipped inside. "You do realize…" he started to say.

"—that we're in an apocalypse?" The Mechanic gave him a side-eye glare. "No shit."

"Then, why?"

"I don't know. Why do we breathe, Limey?"

Hugh rubbed his temples. "That name isn't as insulting as you suspect it is."

The Mechanic's smile grew wolfish. "Fine. How's Fuck-If-I-Care? That work for you?"

Somewhere in the back of his consciousness, Hugh heard Amos laughing, the kind of laugh where his eyes would water. Genuine tears of joy. He'd have enjoyed this back and forth far too much.

"You see, while the publishing industry has all but collapsed along with everything else, there is still such a thing as the Underground." The Mechanic slumped into his desk chair, the cylinder dropping him down a half an inch under his weight and the casters clicking slightly. "You ever hear of it, Fiic?"

"What did you call me?"

"It's short for Fuck-If-I-Care. Don't get hung up on it. Art is art. Those of us with creative bones still need to move them somehow. Maybe even you, Limey. The Underground is accessible everywhere. Free. Like those old chatrooms. Like Myspace. Tumblr. Livejournal. Hell, Reddit. Some people use it to push viruses. With some people, it's agendas. Some people use it to deliver messages they know their dead loved ones will never see. Or some, like me, want to have an escape. So, they follow the adventures of Detective Rex Rink."

Hugh sighed. Not a sitcom sigh. Not an exhausted sigh. It was a sigh in remembrance of that thing he used to be. The thing that had left behind art. Left behind color. Left behind expressionism. Left behind musicality. In its place was the machine: the thing that recognized the end result but couldn't grasp the configuration, that refused to feel. And the refusal to feel was to ignore how art became.

He was blank.

He was numb.

And this was how it needed to be.

The Mechanic watched him and maybe something crossed Hugh's face as that sigh came and went. Maybe nothing at all. Maybe it was the nothing that made the Mechanic get up from his chair and offer it to Hugh.

He stared at it a moment before he cleared his throat. "Petrol."

The Mechanic rolled his eyes and left the office, Hugh stepping aside to let him. "Fine. If that's how you want to live your life."

"You think anyone wants to live this way?" Hugh said before he could stop himself.

The Mechanic leaned over a pile of cardboard boxes into the shadows and pulled out jerry can. "Things are harder. But you're still in charge of you, Fiic. Aren't you?"

"Keep your stitched-on-a-pillow wisdom to yourself," Hugh remarked as he accepted the can. It was empty. Before he could ask, the Mechanic pointed to the old gas pumps out front. "Fill 'er up yourself. And Fiic?"

Hugh glanced back over his shoulder.

"Next time, it won't be free."

The Mechanic sauntered back to work on his truck and Hugh braced himself for the singe of daylight before leaving the shadows of the garage.

# MAL VERDUGO

THE SUN IS GOING DOWN, its burn now extinguished beneath the buildings. The sky has dimmed into a strange green color with orange nuzzled by the horizon line. It'll be dark soon.

The boy watches him from outside his car window, determination set like carvings in stone.

*Bloody fucking hell.*

Hugh reaches across the passenger seat, ignoring the ghastly figure of Amos and opens the passenger door. "Get in," he says.

The kid is hesitant. "I don't even know you."

"That didn't bother you a moment ago when you came to my car window."

Still, he remains where he is, though his eyes are locked on that open door. "Do you know how we can find my sister?"

"I may have some ideas of where to start." Hugh nudges his head to the door again. "Quickly before I change my mind."

The kid rounds the front of the Mercedes and assumes the void left in Amos's wake. He shuts the door with a hollow clunk. "Okay," he murmurs. "Where do we start?"

Hugh puts the car in gear and presses the clutch and gas pedals. "We start in the bazaar. We'll go from there." The car bumps over the gravelly road, down the lane, as neon lights glide across its exterior.

"What's your name?" the kid asks. It sounds like he's trying to be casual, as casual as one can be in this place, among these people.

"Hugh."

The kid scoffs.

"What's so funny?"

"Nothing." He keeps laughing. "It's just that—that's such a British sounding name."

Distantly, perhaps from the backseat, Hugh hears wind rustle through trash in the foot space and it sounds like Amos's chuckle.

# MONTHS AGO

The Tower awaited him in the heart of Nothingland. The glass spire stood unlit in the night save for the top floor which blazed orange like a pagan candle. Hugh parked the stolen car in the empty lot and passed the armed soldiers at the entrance who didn't even twitch to acknowledge him.

He held his breath and when the bile began to rise, he swallowed it back down. He was about to deliver bad news. Better to not smell vile. Steele would think he'd lost his nerve. He had no use for muscle that couldn't stomach death. Though he wasn't sure what there was even left to live for, the split-second worm of terror wriggling in the back of his brain told him he wasn't ready to die yet and certainly not like this.

The bank of elevators were in the back of the spacious, empty lobby. Only a nightwatchman stood at a centralized desk glaring into the light of security camera screens.

The last elevator on the right brought Hugh up to the top floor, to the flaming eye that glared out upon Nothingland like something from a fantasy novel. God, maybe Steele was a formless evil when no one was looking, corrupting the hearts of everyone he influenced. Perhaps that would make it easier to hate him. But, Hugh knew too well that Steele was flesh and blood:

his greed and his thirsts for sadism made it so.

Before it was a resort that then swallowed the entire city it was based in, Nothingland was Steele's brainchild, invented to continue his career monopolies.

Such was the way of Hollywood. Actors who struck it rich with a blockbuster, then continued to garner the favor of the elite, of the fans, of the academies and guilds until their name was synonymous with success. They desperately branched their persona out into at least a dozen other ventures in the off-chance that the next movie might be their worst. Releasing a pop album. Starting a winery. Opening a club. Becoming an ambassador to a noble-sounding cause by a highly pretentious brand.

But Steele was not a lucky man. He was calculated. He planned and organized and executed down to the last unlikely eventuality. His persistence made everything he reached his fingers into turn to fucking gold. So, it only made sense that when the world fell apart, this place grew into something that flourished beyond what was expected of it. It became a way of life and it enveloped whatever it came in contact with, added whatever distinctiveness those things had to its own nightmarish identity. Nothingland became everything.

The elevator opened into a foyer, black marble tiles guiding him down a featureless hall into a room. A blaze flickered and tumbled in the gas fireplace to his right, the only light in the otherwise blackened space. Hugh's senses curled and rippled with the flame, unsure what to expect but knowing full-well this meeting wasn't going to end with a cup of tea and biscuits.

Steele came out of the darkness with the swiftness of any man who assumed their guest had night-vision, with brusqueness. He knocked back his whiskey and cast the empty glass onto the coffee table. He picked up something discarded on the armchair—Hugh squinted—a suit jacket. As he swung it on, he spoke, "You found her, I take it?"

Hugh rolled back his shoulders, fought every molecule inside that desired violence and said, "Just where I thought she'd be: in Axy Gable."

Steele side-eyed him. The blueness of that eye felt alien in the extreme warmth of the room, warmth that sunk through Hugh's sand-covered clothes to his flesh. "Not even trying to hide?"

"She found a man to act as her bodyguard in return for sex. He was collateral damage."

Steele cocked his head but there was no reaction in his face, as if he'd expected she'd do exactly what she did. He walked into the shadows on the other side of the room and moments later, a desk lamp clicked on. He gathered a glittering watch from a leather catch-all dish. "What did she do with the money? Any of it left?"

"Nothing. Blew it all on jewelry, clothing, and skin care."

Steele exhaled and finished securing his cufflinks. "How was her scream?"

Hugh swallowed.

*Here it comes.* Amos's murmur was so crisp in his ear, it made the hairs on the back of his neck stand.

Steele looked up expectantly. "Shrill right? I thought it might have been grating."

"A bit." Hugh leaned into the expectation. "Like a cocker spaniel whining." He waited for the rush of Steele's anger to wash over him like a gale as it charged down a steep hill. He'd know it was a lie. He'd know.

Steele smiled. "Was it?"

He blinked. Nothing? Was his boss buying it? He allowed himself to smile back. "A bit."

Hugh's heart clenched in his chest like a vice. Breath stolen, body locked in rigor, he slammed onto the floor. Black pain lanced through his arteries, surged in flashes from his heart. He clawed a hand at his chest in a pathetic attempt to stop it.

"Lying never suited you," Steele said, no doubt still fastening his cufflinks. Moments later, when he stepped into view over him, it was with a vacancy of care, his mouth scrunched up in a vague "you-asked-for-it" way. "After what happened the first time, I thought it best to send someone to make sure you could actually get the job done."

Convulsing, Hugh twitched his eyes to the second figure as she revealed herself from the shadows. She sat in the armchair by the fire, her hand squeezing the air as if choking an invisible rabbit. Her fingers twisted more and whatever air Hugh thought he had summoned to say something shriveled out of him in a whimper.

"I'm tired of having these kinds of talks," Steele murmured as he crouched down close to Hugh. "So, let's not do this again. When I tell you to find someone, when I tell you to make them suffer, it isn't an option. It's not for you to decide who's granted mercy, you understand?"

His vision blurring, Hugh swore he saw a shape reflected in the shadows over Steele's head, the shape familiar, the stance one he knew from another life. Amos? He wanted to reach for it, but every muscle screamed in protest.

"You understand?" Steele repeated.

Foam rippled from between his lips, the bubbles popping against his skin. Heart strangled, Hugh forced his chin into the air, the closest thing he could do to nod.

"Say it."

An exhale. "I…*ugh*… under…*guk*…stand."

Steele waved his fingers and the Witch opened her hand.

His heart thrashing in his chest, pulse reverberating in his head, Hugh gasped to force all the air into his lungs that he could. Sweat poured down his forehead as he scraped his fingers across the fabric of his shirt.

Somewhere in between his vision winnowing and then sling-shotting back into focus, Steele had moved to the hallway behind him to collect his coat. "The Witch will introduce your next mark. You're to bring whatever recompense they have back. And Hugh?"

Hugh struggled to curl into a sitting position, to glance back over his shoulder.

"I want it messy this time." Steele didn't wait for confirmation before he sauntered down the hall to the elevator and vanished from sight within moments.

The Witch stood from her chair, delicate fingers plucking a tissue from the box on the coffee table. She let it sail like an autumn leaf onto his lap as she said, "Clean yourself up and meet me downstairs, Maestro." The heels of her boots clicked away down the hall.

Hugh dabbed at the lingering foam on his lips, the tissue coming back pink.

# DEPRESSION

# BEFORE

"You know something?"

Hugh turned to look at Amos. "What's that, love?" The sky was becoming deep blue outside and only the soft light over the sink bathes them.

"This is our first date anniversary." He said it as he tilted his head, hand scrubbing circles on the plate he was cleaning. The hot water made a beautiful rushing sound, like white noise in the emptiness between their words.

"Huh… So it is." Hugh's reaction was as blithe as Amos's.

His partner smiled and turned back to the dishes.

Hugh absently wrung the dishtowel in his hands. "Should we…do something?"

"I don't know. Do you want to?" So casual, the way he used to drop subtleties. He did. He wanted to do something but he didn't want to be the one to suggest the idea. Amos really was crafty that way. Always setting things up like a cat plotting a strategy to be given cream.

So, Hugh gave it back to him. "We could… If you want to."

Amos eyed him for a moment before squinting. Just as he was about to open his mouth, Hugh continued, "…Or I suppose we don't have to. We could just finish the dishes and then, maybe turn in early? Or perhaps there's something we could throw on the telly?"

Amos winced, as if he were trying to hold back the discomfort of an upset stomach. It made Hugh nearly break character, a small snort expelling from his nose at the sight.

"You—!" Amos's smile exploded onto his face. He lobbed the fully loaded sponge at Hugh and he wasn't fast enough to turn away before it splatted against his chest. Chuckling, Hugh turned the dishtowel into a whip and caught Amos across the ass with it. Amos turned the sink sprayer on him and hit him with a luke-warm blast. They ended up in each other's arms, giggling and kissing.

"So," Amos asked him when the laughs abated. "Did you want to do something?"

"Unbelievable," Hugh answered, trying not to crack a smile. "Why are you like this?"

"Well, if I were anyone else, you wouldn't like me as much as you do." He grinned.

"That's fair."

"Admit it: you love—"

The elevator doors opened. Hugh snapped back to the here and now. Emotion straight-jacketed into place again, memory switched off. He focused on the details of the lobby as he stepped into it, eyes narrowing on the Witch's figure near the doors to the parking lot. He swallowed, head still pounding.

She smoked, the cigarette's fume hazy around her. It was only in the few moments before she noticed him that he saw her mask slip. Anger that was brighter than any usual nuisance she used to cover it. He wondered what lay deeper beneath it. What had she lost in the fall of the world? How had she come to be…this?

The Witch saw him and flicked the half-spent cigarette into the ash tray nearby. "Took you long enough," she grumbled, fishing a phone out from her bag once he was close enough. She tossed it to him and he caught it deftly, keeping a couple feet between them.

"Dodgers," he said, powering on the burner phone.

"It always is." She scrutinized the floor as though she were trying to divine something in the crisscrossing patterns of its tiles. "It's never going to end."

His eyes flicked to hers before returning to the phone. "It has to at some point. There can't be too many left."

"You know how many people he's leant money to?" The darkness of her eyeshadow made her eyes whiter in the dimness of their surroundings. She looked possessed and it sent a chill down his spine into his feet. "Even people who didn't need it. Greed is irresistible. Steele knows it. He doesn't care if he gets any of it back. It's like he's giving them a test he knows they won't pass."

Hugh leered at her. "It's never been about the money; it's about the punishment. Their pain is theatrical for him."

The Witch's eyes narrowed to slits. "If you keep fucking up, he's going to turn his violence closer to home. He's going to take it out on all of us. I didn't put myself in this position just so you could ruin everything."

Hugh scoffed. "Don't tell me you're worried about him. You could snap his neck like a pencil if you wanted whenever you'd like."

The Witch cackled. The kind of laugh Hugh remembered someone from the PTA having back when he used to take his daughter to public school.

*No.*

He slashed the thought from his mind.

*You don't have a daughter anymore.*

Here. Now. Present.

"You think so?" the Witch kept going. "You don't understand his power then. You don't understand his reach. He's like a shadow sliding along the wall. He's unstoppable."

"Yet you stand at his side unleashing hell on whoever he points to."

"You think what happened upstairs hurt?" She sneered. "I could have made your heart feel like it was boiling in acid. I could have made you beg like a fool as I tied your insides in a knot. I went easy on you, Hugh. I won't next time."

"How can you still work for him after everything he's done? He's a monster."

"We're all monsters." She shook her head. "What mercy you think you granted that girl he sent you to kill? It's still violence: undeserved, brutal… and permanent."

His heart drummed against his ribs. Breath rattled in and out of him as he fought the urge to say something baiting, to get her to kill him right then and there.

*No.*

*The pain is all we have left of them.*

*And Ella's still...* He wouldn't let himself think it but deep inside, the heaviness breathed and lifted. *Out there somewhere. Keep going.*

"So, because we're aware of our own savagery, it means we have no control over it?" he said slowly, more asking than anything. He wasn't sure there was a point left to prove.

"Savagery is just a part of nature," the Witch said, stubbing out her cigarette against the nearest wall and stepping through the glass doors into the night.

He followed.

"You don't ask a fox why it tears the mouse apart. It's just doing what it needs to survive."

"Empathy is as natural as cruelty," Hugh said.

"In socialized animals." She turned to him, her body backlit by the streetlamps over the sidewalk. Behind her, Nothingland's buildings vanished into the bleak darkness of midnight. "We're all alone here, Maestro. Everything we do is purely for our own survival. Even your attempts at mercy killing."

She left, dematerializing into the black.

# MAL VERDUGO

T HE KID TELLS HIM HIS NAME and Hugh lets it sink into the mire of noise outside the car as he concentrates on the road ahead. The kid's name doesn't matter. All he is in those moments now is The Mark: the one who Steele sent him to kill. The one who would lead him to his sister so he could end their lives together. That was how this was going to end and the personal details were of no concern because it was going to end the same way all the others had. There was no room for error.

When Hugh doesn't answer, the Mark focuses on himself, zips up his ragged navy sweatshirt and pulls his sleeves down over his hands. It makes it seem as though he's being swallowed by all the loose fabric. It's too big on him. Perhaps it had fit at one time. But the Mark is scrawny, likely from not eating. Likely from spending day and night travelling.

The dossier said the brother and sister were from outside of Pria. That's two states away. Steele's intel said the Mark had been on the road searching for his sister for longer than four days. Weeks hunting, scavenging for food… Hugh is amazed the kid is still upright and speaking, let alone moving.

*"Desperation does that to you,"* Amos says from the back seat. *"You know that."*

"You said we were going to the bazaar?" The Mark asks, finally breaking out of his shell of tire. "What's that?"

"Call it the artery of Mal Verdugo," Hugh says. "Anyone who's anyone has set foot there and will likely have seen her. Will know where she's gone."

It is the truth and a lie together. Hugh is almost certain he knows where the girl is, or rather who she is with. But finding them is just as difficult. And he wants to be sure.

They follow the avenue for a ways, slowing down and occasionally stopping for pedestrians in the roadway, some who race to be out of sight and others who take their time crossing with their shopping carts and rolling duffels of belongings.

The shuffle: this city is all about it now. The sidewalks become exhibitions of squalor in the nighttime, with the meek and the trifling selling or bartering whatever they can for a scrap of food, a warm blanket, a roof over their heads to protect them from the vicious sun in the day.

"It's worse out here than I ever imagined." The Mark's voice is merely an echo of its earlier bravado. "I saw some of the stories on the news back when there was still news… But I never thought it was like this."

"Is this your first time away from home?" Again, Hugh doesn't actually care. But it seems as though the Mark wants to talk and if talk keeps him at ease, keeps him from peering past the mask Hugh wears until the job is done, then that was what the job would take.

"I was finishing up my masters when Ruby called me. Told me Mom was sick. I spent the last two years at home trying to take care of her, of them… My uncle owned a small organic food store in town so we had supplies for a while. But the medicine that Mom needed…" The Mark peers into the pit near his feet, his eyes watering. "I'm not proud of my decision but it kept her with us for a little longer. That was all that mattered."

Hugh doesn't need for him to explain. He'd borrowed money: Steele's money. He's heard the story over and over countless times through the years only this time, for some reason, he's sick, like a noxious cloud is slowly eating away at him from the inside.

*"He's just like you,"* Amos's voice says from the darkness behind him. *"Isn't that something?"*

*Of course he is,* Hugh thinks. *And there are hundreds just like him. Thousands forced to take out loans or remortgage homes, sell priceless heirlooms, property, necessities, all so that they didn't have to watch their loved ones suffer…*

"*You didn't watch,*" Amos cautions. "*You weren't there.*"

Hugh abruptly turns the car onto a side street, away from the lights, away from the reminders of broken humanity. Newspapers and shiny candy wrappers skitter across the roadway in the windy twilight. The road slopes down and turns the color of absinthe in the glare of green neon as they snake their way along.

"No father?" Hugh asks the Mark.

"No. Last I heard from him, he was shacking up with his third wife in Obsolescence: a stripper named Taffi Streamers. That was when I was in high school."

The dad had since dumped Taffi, built up enormous amounts of debt with a collector in Reels City and had died in a hit and run outside of his local bodega, the Wet Whistle. The Mark knew none of that though, clearly. It was all in the file Hugh had received from Steele; someone had kept an exhaustive eye on anyone the Mark could run to if he were looking to hide.

Hugh glances at his passenger. It is odd that the Mark is all too trusting in his new companion when he's overdue to pay a loan that borders in the realm of over fifty thousand dollars. It's almost as if he doesn't care.

"*Well…*" Amos speaks again. "*He doesn't.*"

He's concerned with finding his sister. He'd left his educational ambitions behind to go home and care for his mother. He borrowed money he couldn't pay back because he'd been desperate. Family is everything. Family is all that matters.

Hugh stops the car near the end of the street and pulls up the parking brake. "We'll be better off going on foot from here," he says. "We don't want to spook them."

In the faint glow of lights, he sees the Mark's lips part in question. "Who?"

"The acolytes."

MONTHS AGO

Coffee: it somehow melded the world together for Americans. Hugh had warmed to it, spurred on by Amos's appreciation for it. But in the days since his partner's death, in the years without him, tea rippled back in and filled the emptiness that drinking coffee produced. What was an Englishman without his tea after all?

That evening at the Pancake House was no exception to any of the others he'd spent there. He sat at one of the tables along the wall, a cup of black tea with sugar in an off-white diner mug and a plate of potato wedges in front of him. Maybe he'd eat them. Maybe not. If he could turn off the—

*"You want to try it?" Hugh tipped the coffee mug toward Ella.*

*She stretched her neck to look inside, eyes full of stars, of wonder. "What is it?"*

*"It's made from magic beans," Amos called from the laundry room. He was folding clothes. The aroma of fresh linen spilled out into the hall.*

*Ella's brows came down. "It looks dirty."*

*Hugh shrugged. "I suppose it is."*

*She looked at him. "Is it made from dirty beans?"*

*He smiled so hard his cheeks hurt. Amos laughed from the other room. "When you're older, you'll understand."*

"Morning, Hugh," Silkie said. The waitress brushed by the table on her way to deliver a plate of pancakes to a man who sat by himself a couple of booths down. Hugh's vision trails after her. She was in her forties, dark hair twisted up at the back of her head, her apron covered in coffee stains and grease. She looked tired. It had clearly been a busy night.

*Amos poked his head out of the laundry room door. "She's going to be a coffee gremlin. You wait."*

He didn't answer Silkie.

*"That's just what you'd like, isn't it?" he called back. "Then it would be two against one."*

He didn't eat his potatoes.

*"But I converted you," Amos said matter-of-factly. "You're one of us!"*

*Ella's face scrunched up. "I don't like it!"*

*"You haven't even tried it!" Hugh leaned the cup toward her a little more. "Here, smell it. See what you—"*

He took a long sip of his tea as his throat began to close up. As the burning started in the corners of his eyes. He filled his mouth with liquid until it was almost bursting and swallowed hard, the tea scorching as it coursed down his throat. It distracted him. Just for a moment. It was all he needed.

He was close to tears. "Sweetheart. Sweetheart. Come on. Let's read the book together."

She was sobbing, hiding under her blanket. It was her favorite one: the yellow one, woven with soft angora yarn. Amos had picked it out for her before she was even born.

"No!" Her voice squealed. "You're not reading it right. You never read it right!" At least, that's what he thought she said. Her words come out garbled and snot-filled. She cried so hard, she took great weeping breaths in between her words. He imagined a willow tree assaulted by a storm with every cough.

No. He wasn't reading it the same way that Amos did. It was their favorite story and he'd read it to her almost every night for the last six months.

But Amos was asleep. He needed to be asleep. Ever since they'd gotten home from their trip to the beach, he'd been strange. Dazed. Not himself. He'd gone to bed early complaining of being exhausted and Hugh wanted nothing more than to give his husband the rest he needed. The hour-long drive had felt like it took forever and Ella was difficult through it to say the least.

She was over-tired. They'd stayed up watching an animated movie she'd been looking forward to seeing, something he'd used to distract her after the awkwardness of their car ride back. She'd wanted to stop and see the lighthouse like they'd done in the past but instead, they'd gone straight home.

"You're right," he acquiesced, taking a tight breath. "So, let's read a different book then."

"But…" She poked her head out from beneath the blanket, face red and eyes puffy. "But-but… I want this one." There were tiny droplets at the ends of her lashes, like dew on grass. His girl. This was how he knew. She cried all the time. Just like he had when he was her age.

He cleared his throat. "Then you'll have to settle for me—"

Darkness.

Faint banging sounds from above.

Where—

It slammed into him: the musty smell, the closeness of the walls, his heavy breathing.

He knew. But—

*She sat there, the yellow blanket draped around her shoulders, bottom lip trembling as she nodded—*

Distant shouting.

The kitchen upstairs. It was the shift change, morning crew coming into relieve the graveyard cooks. Even though he was directly below, the smell of pancakes and waffles, bacon and coffee didn't permeate the thick walls or carry down the stairs to the tiny room.

He wished it would for once.

Why?

Because it was a distraction. Because it would keep him from thinking about—

*Ella scooted closer to him on the bed, her knee brushing his thigh. "Why did daddy go to bed early?"*

Something unclenched in his throat. He struggled to swallow it back down. Wads of cotton were being pushed through his chest up through his esophagus. He couldn't breathe through it.

*"Your father had a long day."* Hugh *forced himself to smile, the corners of his lips straining. "He'll be as right as rain tomorrow."*

He flung himself up from the mattress, hanging over its side as he shouted: not a word, not a cry or a roar. Something undefinable that glided out of him like sheets of smoke through a cracked window. He took a short breath before another grunt was purged.

The darkness of that room was absolute, a canvas his memory could paint on too easily to pull back the past. He could see his daughter's room, its coral-colored walls, yellow lights, pale blue sheets. He could feel the faint gusts of summer wind caressing him through the cracked window…

He opened his eyes. It was the air vent. Just the heat.

In the dark, he found the nearest switch for a lamp and turned it on. The room bloomed the color of afternoon. He stared at the old metal desk against the wall beside his cot, at the emptiness of it. In the bottom right-hand drawer were a mess of objects he'd cobbled together from his former life, random things he'd taken with him in that dead of morning when he'd left her…

A drawer he hadn't opened in years.

Other than that, that desk was useless. The only reason it was still there was because it was a bitch to have to move it. It must have weighed close to a hundred and fifty pounds. Not worth toting it up a flight of steep stairs to get rid of it. What would he even put in its place?

He changed clothes and checked his bag. Nothing to restock. His small med kit was still full. He added a clean shirt to the mix this time. After a moment, added clean briefs and socks, too.

*The next place he was off to is even hotter than the last.*

Coffee. Blasted coffee.

There was something about it he needed that morning. Like taking a sip would put a smile on the memory of Amos. It was strange: the need to satisfy a ghost, a whisp. But he didn't care. It was the closest thing to bringing him back that he could muster right then.

*"Smells good,"* Amos said as he sat on the stool beside him. He was

wearing that dark blue button down that Hugh had loved. "What kind of roast is it?"

How the bloody hell should he know? He shrugged.

*"I was only asking,"* Amos murmured.

*I'm sure it's whatever they could find*, he thought. *Whatever bottom of the barrel bags they cobbled together from some factory somewhere. No one's importing beans anymore.*

*"So, that means that someday, the coffee will run out?"*

*Yes*, Hugh thought. *Inevitably.*

Amos stared down at the counter, no longer smiling. *"Suppose it's good I'm not around after all, huh?"*

"You'd never survive." Hugh took a long drink, the roof of his mouth scalding. "Kind people don't survive now."

"Hugh?"

He looked up. Mandy was this waitress's name. She had red highlights in her shiny dark hair. Confusion pulled at her eyebrows as she filled a new coffee pot full of water.

"It's nothing," he told her. He left the rest of the mug behind, left the Pancake House, and climbed into the stolen car on the street out front. He waited until he was a few blocks from the Pancake House to thump a fist against his chest, against his heart as hard as he could. Maybe it would stop beating. Maybe he could cheat his way out of Steele's service? Maybe he expected something to knock back? As if Amos were locked inside somehow…

But nothing did.

"All you have to do is agree." Steele had been nothing more than a man in a fancy suit then, a stranger who had summoned him to the meeting room of a luxury hotel by name with just a phone call. "I'm aware of your particular talents, Hugh. Both the music you use to serenade and the backwoods magic that you practice. You do this one job for me and this could cement you with a more steady source of income. You understand what I'm saying."

He did. Amos had only been diagnosed a few months ago. The hospital had recommended routine visits, physical therapy, psychological evaluations, in-home care... That cost money. Lots of money.

But he'd heard of Steele. He'd heard rumors of people taking his charity and vanishing. He didn't want any part of it. And, he had his own treatments that he and Amos were going to try. Herbal ones. Magical ones. They'd solve this together without the need to get into debt.

"I'm sure that little girl of yours could use some new dollies or hell, put some money in an account for college." Steele's eyes bore holes into his.

Hugh shivered. "No."

Steele chuckled. "No, what?"

"I'm not interested." He tried to say it as respectfully as possible, even taking a step back while keeping his eyes on him. "Sorry to have wasted your time."

"Not a waste at all," Steele answered as he walked him to the door and saw him out. "Let me know when you reconsider. The door is always open for a talent like you."

# BARGAINING

# MAL VERDUGO

THEY GET OUT OF THE CAR and follow the sidewalk down to the corner. The Bazaar is a square of lurid giddiness. Thriving with chaos, with the skimpily clad and the jewelry draped, the mystified, the enamored, and the lurkers. Hugh has never been to Mal Verdugo but he ventures it is like most cities that come alive at nighttime after the Collapse: that people still roam and move about in vaguely antiparallel lines along sidewalks, crossing the street where they ought to, staying in the light, hypnotized by the plethora of visual incitements.

Those worse off cling to the shadows and the crevices where they can't become targets, where they might find a fellow sufferer with something to trade.

The Bazaar is entertainment personified: the place where those who have stolen their wealth flaunt it, where the performers who can still earn a living by their skills execute street performances; where the sexual appetites abound as men and women and all those in between offer their bodies; for the hustlers and the gamblers and the pimps to skitter and linger and watch for potential victims.

In essence, this place hasn't changed much save for its notable absence of an authority presence.

When Hugh looks back, he sees the Mark lost in awe of the spectacle around them, his eyes ever drifting from one lighted sign to the next.

"Put your hands in your pockets," Hugh advises him.

"Why?"

"To make sure no one else's end up there."

"I don't have anything for them to steal." The scuffing of shoes on the sidewalk brings the Mark up next to Hugh as he tries to match his speed. "What acolytes are we looking for?"

"In a crowd this size? They'll find us."

Hugh scans the throng they walk with. The smells of sweet perfume, the tang of cheap beer, and clouds of cigarette smoke so potent, they nearly make him want to divert his course. But, if they separate themselves to stand back and watch, they will be more noticeable. Best to blend in, make themselves look like every other idiot in the Bazaar.

At first, there is just the shuffle, the occasional stop and go as crowds gather around a busker performing with a badly-tuned guitar or two contortionists gyrating their bodies in insane ways that make them appear to be rubber, like those toys Ella used to play with years ago.

Heat assaults his face as he desperately tries to force back the visions of her, of her small hands in his, of her stubborn mouth watching him, judging him that last day they'd spent together. Everywhere he looks, he can see her in the crowd, the pink of her winter jacket vanishing between swishing legs and flailing arms.

And then, Amos: standing in front of him, his eyes pools of gravity that draw Hugh in. *"Shhh. It's okay. It's okay."* His delicate hands wrap around Hugh's face, fingers gently stroking his temples. *"I've got you. You're—"*

"—safe in our hands."

The words bubble against Hugh's psyche, yank him from the torrent of sadness into the lights and the color and the confusion. He looks up at the hooded figure standing opposite them, a crumpled stack of fliers in her hand, her fingers extending one to a couple of lost looking girls in front of them in the crowd. It hits him how white her skin is, eerily so in the midst of a mostly sunbaked people. The hood over her face keeps him from seeing her features but there's something deeply soothing about her voice, almost like listening to honey drip from the tip of a spoon.

"Are you okay?" The Mark asks him, his tone wavering.

"There." Hugh tilts his head toward the woman in the crowd. "You stay on my heels."

The woman parts from the two girls, an almost dance-like smoothness to her movements as she pivots and slips through the public like a ribbon.

Hugh locks his eyes on her as she crosses the road and follows suit. He won't let her out of his sight—can't. He's sure the Mark is following; the scuffing of his once-white Chuck Taylors on the pavement is enough to assure him.

She sidles through a crowd gathered to watch a vaudevillian clown performing with knives, before her hood is lost from sight behind tall and stout figures.

Hugh picks up his pace, throwing himself into the throng, hands shoving people aside, fingers pressing into someone's neck, palm catching another's cheek. She *can't* get away. He can't *let* her.

There! There she goes, disappearing into an alley between buildings.

Breaking away from the crowd, Hugh closes in on it only to catch the frightened yelp of his companion from behind. Whirling around, he sees a bearded behemoth manhandling the Mark back into the crowd.

Charging into the fray once more, Hugh's tongue is already moving as he lifts a hand and casually flicks it. The brute careens off his feet and into the clown juggling knives. People put their hands up to their mouths, gasp, and laugh, and shriek—he's not sure if it's in delight or fear.

Grabbing the Mark by his arm, Hugh hauls him out of the flurry of people and over beneath the tattered awning of a nearby hotel.

"I told you to stay on my heels!"

The Mark gasps, trying to catch his breath. "You were going too fast... And then that guy just came out of nowhere!"

Hugh is only half-listening, his attention back on the alley where the hooded woman vanished. He sticks his head into it but sees nothing: no movement, no figures hiding in its depths. "Fuck," he says through gritted teeth.

"Why did you chase her? What the fuck is going on?" The Mark whines.

Hugh tracks his gaze back to the opposite side of the road. "Where did those girls go?"

"What girls?"

"The ones she gave the pamphlet to." He can't see them. He's lost them as well.

"Wha—What? Please, can you just talk to me? Can you just tell me what—"

Hugh snatches the scruff of his sweater. "You want to find your sister, don't you? Stop asking so many bloody questions. Jesus." He thrusts him away.

The Mark half-stumbles but catches himself before he falls. "Hey! I don't have to take this! I'll find her on my own." He turns to walk away.

*You're going to lose him,* Amos says.

Hugh notices him standing at the edge of the crowd, hands in his pockets, mouth a straight line.

"He's going to get himself killed either way," Hugh blusters.

*"And if you don't do it, Steele will make sure your death hurts like hell before you go."* Amos's face twists in concern. *"You can't let it end like this, Hugh."*

"Fuck if I—" He looks after the Mark as he gets further down the sidewalk. This was stupid. He couldn't let this one boy and his sister influence his existence. He had to make sure they were both killed. He needed to do it. He couldn't let it all be...

*"Que Sera Sera."*

Hugh looks to where Amos was standing and instead finds a rubbish bin. On top is a half-crumpled flier. He can barely read the words near the top: "Embrace the new you!"

"—Fuck." He grabs it from the bin and starts down the sidewalk. "Wait!"

The Mark glances over his shoulder.

Hugh walks to him before he says, "I believe your sister is with Elixir."

The Mark frowns. "What's that?"

"Come on. I'll explain on the way."

The two of them saunter back in the direction of the parked Mercedes.

# BEFORE

"Hugh!"

He almost didn't hear Amos calling for him. The greenhouse was only ten feet from the back patio door but once he was inside it amidst the sea of plants and beneath the thick plastic, he might as well have been in another world. *Que Sera Sera* played from the turntable in the living room, wafting on the air like the smell of bittersweet.

Moments later, Amos appeared in the doorway, urgency alight in his eyes. "What are you doing out here? Come on! We're going to be late!"

Something turned in Hugh's gut. Shit. He'd forgotten something, hadn't he? What were they supposed to do that day? "Damn!" He dropped his clippers, pulled off his gloves and followed Amos toward the house. Where was Ella? He wasn't sure. Last he saw her, she was playing in the backyard near the firewood stack but she was no longer there.

"We should have left ages ago!" Amos lamented as he hurried to their bedroom, Hugh in tow.

"For what? What did I miss?"

"Sally's birthday party! Remember? She's never going to forgive us!"

"Sally's…" Hugh's brow crinkled. "Sally McPearson?"

"Who else?" Amos yanked open the bureau drawer. "You really *did* forget."

"Didn't she move away? To Tolgate or something?"

Amos turned to him and shook his head. "Where'd you get that idea?" He redoubled his efforts in searching the drawers. "Help me find my shirt. The nice navy one with the buttons?"

Hugh swallowed. "Amos, we got rid of that one. Remember? It had that stain we couldn't get out."

Amos straightened. Panic had settled on his brow now. "What? How could we get rid of it? I don't—"

"Amos." Hugh put a hand on his arm. "The last time we talked to Sally was something like ten years ago."

Amos's mouth puckered, straightened. Puckered, straightened. His eyebrows were eternally furrowed. "No. That's—that's not…"

"You're starting to scare me," Hugh murmured. "Come sit down for a moment?"

They sat on the end of the bed.

"I don't know…" Amos stared at his lap. "I don't know why I was so convinced. I just really thought…"

"Are you feeling alright? Should we call—"

"I'm fine." His voice was shaky.

"I'm not convinced, darling."

As Amos opened his mouth, Ella ran into the room, her face full of glee. "I have to show you something!" She grabbed at Amos's hand and tugged. "Please! Please!"

Hugh saw the micro-adjustment on Amos's face before he leapt up and followed her. It was confusion. Full-throated confusion.

He stood in the middle of their bedroom, listening to the sounds of his husband and daughter echoing down the hall, to the sound of Doris Day gleefully singing away on the speaker and shivered.

# MONTHS AGO

HE'D KISSED A BOY on the garden path outside the academy at fourteen. It was spring, the ground sodden by a recent rain, fuchsia tulips popping against clusters of daffodils. Froths from the weeping willows trailed down over them like dripping clouds of pale green, blocking the sun and the sight of other students. Hugh even remembered his name—Dennis. He wondered if Dennis were even still alive in this cracked and hardened shell of what the world used to be.

Probably not. Dennis had been too soft.

Hugh thought of his younger self: eyes bright, nerves buzzing like dragonfly wings as they just looked after one another, not sure what to do next. And even as the excitement caught up with him, fear latched on with larger teeth. Fear his brother might have seen him. Fear his father might find out. Fear of what others might do or think or say…

He'd taken Dennis's hand and tried to lead him further into the garden. He knew a few paces more would bring them to a place where they could be lost amongst the irises and the hyacinths and the hellebore.

But it was Dennis who resisted. Dennis who shook his head as his eyes welled up and it was Dennis who retreated back to the front of the school with a meek, "I'm sorry."

Hugh couldn't blame Dennis all these years later. At the time, he was adrift: bestowed with a revelation about himself only to be left crushed and uncertain.

They never experimented again after that, barely said a word to one another all through school. And Dennis always cast him this hopeful glance from across rooms or halls that Hugh would break.

He had never been a "fool me twice" person. Risk often always came with disappointment, with pain. Why take a chance when the odds weren't on his side?

This mark reminded Hugh of Dennis a lot.

Perhaps too much.

The gawky man with thin wrists, prominent Adam's apple and large flittering brown eyes lived in a hole. Well. The kind of apartment that could be *considered* a hole. The kind of apartment one lived in to hide, to not be noticed. The kind of place that hid the fact that the person living there might have more than what they showed the world.

From the shadows of the backstreet, Hugh watched as the Mark finished eating his supper—something in a bowl—and then turned out all the lights to reveal an emerald glow emanating from deep within. He waited a good ten minutes more before silently entering the complex, toeing up each step of the filthy, smoke stench-filled staircase and standing outside the scuffed apartment door, trying not to be distracted by the flickering lights in the hall.

A tender grasp and wiggle of the doorknob determined it was locked, but more than that, Hugh felt a heat coming from behind it that caught him off guard. Getting inside wasn't too difficult: the lock was old and the door rickety. As it peeled in, the moisture hit him like he imagined a rain forest would feel. Like he remembered those school gardens felt all those years ago.

Even in the verdant darkness, Hugh recognized the aroma of plant-life, the haze of their humidity caressing the skin of his cheeks and his chin, his hands…

"How?" The word dropped from Hugh's lips unintentionally.

There was barely enough water left for humans to survive, vast quantities horded by those with influence, armies, and vicious agendas… How could this small man have enough to—

"Because no one notices me." The voice came from the direction of the window. Hugh had enough time to throw up his hand and mutter a couple words, electricity crackling through his bloodstream as the figure stumbled into him. The acrid stench flared up beneath his nostrils as the Mark choked on his own blood, as the hiss of it kissed Hugh's face in a sprayed mist.

Bright pain.

Hugh staggered, the foreignness of an object sticking into his leg, followed by agony: the kind that oozed rainbows like oil slick.

Hugh dropped a hand on his thigh and his fingers shaped the handle of the fork lodged in the thick muscle there. He gagged. Rivers of hot blood careened down his leg, soaking into his sock, into his shoe.

"Fuck…Fuck!"

He gripped around the neck of the fork and tugged. His stomach swiveled as the meat stuck to the prongs before—*shlock*—

He collapsed on the tiles. In the green lights, Hugh watched a rivulet of blood roll down the curved end of the fork's root.

Only a few feet in front of him, the Mark's body shuddered as his blood boiled him alive from the inside out. Hugh could barely see the steaming of his eye sockets like hot soup as the skin around them bubbled and sagged.

Shaking, he held his hand over the wound in his leg and focused on the only thing that gave him strength: the memory of Amos. The memory of Ella.

A seething at the back of his head wrapped around to his temples and his own blood ignited as more emptied from his leg with the action.

Fuck. He couldn't perform blood magic while bleeding.

Palms against the slick floor, Hugh pulled himself along until he could grasp the seat of a dining table chair to wrestle himself into. The lights for the kitchenette were close enough to tick on with the tip of his finger.

Dark green leaves, ivies, and fronds spawned from almost every opening, pots crowded atop the refrigerator, tiny succulents lined across the range control panel, and edged the puce countertops. On the table in front of him sat a majestic monstera, its wide waxy leaves reaching out to greet him.

Hugh fought back the urge to heave as he cataloged each plant. One of them had to be right. Had to make do to heal…

The notion was silly. None of them *had* to be right. His luck alone stated that they wouldn't be. He'd have to stumble down those stairs, walk the three blocks back to his stolen car and hope he could find some kind of clinic. There had to be one in a city like this—

*"There you go again,"* Amos said. *"What did you just finish telling yourself?"*

"You're not real." Hugh scraped the chair across the floor to the sink, snatched the dish towel slung there and pressed it unrelentingly into the four tiny punctures in his leg. This made the edges of his vision go white.

*"I used to be."*

Hugh tapped the shoe on his opposite foot against the tile, the sound grounding him, distracting him from Amos's voice, from the pain. The next movement was pivoting himself around and pushing back toward the small den. The Mark was wearing a belt. It would have to do.

The body had finally stilled. He unbuckled the belt and slid it haltingly through the loops of the Mark's pants. The light bubbling of blood fizzed from the body's throat as he carefully wrapped the leather around his thigh, threaded the buckle and tightened, not enough to cut off circulation, just enough to hold the towel to his leg.

He collapsed back in the chair swallowing a scream. *Elevate the leg. Try to slow the bleeding.* He propped his foot up on the arm for the sofa.

For the next several minutes, Hugh measured his breaths. He listened to the sounds of air rushing in and out of his own lungs and thought that maybe Dennis did, after all, have the gumption to have survived in this world. Maybe.

If he'd never had that dalliance with Dennis in the garden, he might never have appreciated plants and gardening the same way.

He might never have met Amos.

*"You seem to want to forget about me."*

Hugh opened his eyes, pain shooting to the forefront of his mind. Amos had felt so close in those moments that Hugh was afraid he'd have reached out and tried to touch him. That was a sadness he couldn't feel again.

He needed to go.

As Hugh staggered to the door, he glanced back at the plants one last time. They would wither and die here. Perhaps that was for the best.

"You said we'd never stay here again." Ella's eyes were like flint. He only looked once and couldn't bear to do it again. "You promised."

"I know." Every word he said weighed too much. He busied himself with setting up their tent, what was left of it anyway. One of the poles was broken, bent out of shape, the cord inside losing its elasticity. He struggled to feed the pole through the plastic hooks. A few were broken. The tent drooped sadly on the left side. "We don't have anywhere else to go."

"Why can't we just go back home?" He heard the sob in her voice. "Who cares if the bank owns it? No one is staying there. It would be better than this!"

Because it wasn't safe. Because Steele would find them there. Both of them. Hell, he probably knew where they were at that very moment. He probably was watching their suffering like it was his favorite television show. "We can't go back there, Ella. It's out of the question."

"Hold on!" She stepped into him and her fist socked him in the leg. "Hold—"

"—STILL."

Hugh heaved and as he did, something pinched through his skin. His hands clenched at the leather armrest of the couch he slumped on, fingers scratching at it with every jerk of the needle. Every punch as the tiny piece of metal glided back and forth from one half of the wound to the other.

The doctor didn't flinch. "You made it worse taking it out, you know?"

He wanted to retort. *I can't just go around with a fork sticking out of my leg.* But he made the mistake of looking down. The wound was slick with blood and the smear of lidocaine. A sudden urge to vomit hit him with all the urgency of a softball to the stomach. He watched her mouth move, knew she's talking to him but his hearing had washed out, replaced with a high-pitched whine.

She looked him in the eye and grabbed hold of his shoulder, squeezed it. He read her lips: "Don't move."

He closed his eyes, breathing through his mouth, exhaling through his nose.

"It's your fault!" she screamed at him. "It's your fault!"

His body could crumple into dust right then, be carried away on the next gust of wind. He didn't have the energy to cry. He didn't have the energy to fight back. He was exhausted, starving. And he knew she was right.

If it hadn't been for him, Amos would still be alive.

If it hadn't been for him, they would still have a home.

If it hadn't been for him, they might have been eating actual food and not whatever herbs or scraps they could forage.

If only he had just told Steele 'yes' the first time. Yes, he'd do the job. Yes, he'd take the money. Yes, he'd do more.

Steele didn't like to be told "no."

He'd found out the hard way.

That was why he had to do this now. It was the only way.

He had to say goodbye to her in the only way he knew how: by making her believe he was dead. She'd be safer this way.

"Done."

The green lights of the late-night clinic poured into his eyes once more as he looked down at the mangled, stitched together wound in his leg. The doctor peeled off her dirtied gloves and tossed them into the sink to wash. "Keep it as clean and dry as you can," she said as she rifled through a drawer for a small plastic packet. She handed it to him. "Put the antibiotic on it in about forty-eight hours with a fresh bandage. Watch for signs of infection. Come back to me if that happens."

He nodded though he knew the chance of seeing her again was a hundred to one. He had no plans to return to this place unless he absolutely had to. Who knew if she'd even be here when he did. Quick-fix clinics like this one never stayed put for long.

They stood awkwardly and stared at one another. Payment. It was such a odd exchange now adays that money was essentially useless. Things like medicine, food, and shelter were far more important. And water? It might as well have been the new gold.

Hugh handed her a small card with a phone number on it. "This is somewhere in Nothingland you can go if you need a place to stay. Any time for as long as you need."

Her expression curdled. The card might as well have been writhing with worms. "That horrible place? Ain't nobody ending up there who don't wish they were dead already." She tossed it in a drawer. "Get out of here."

# MAL VERDUGO

"Wait, wait, wait... Say that one more time." The Mark pinches the bridge of this nose in the passenger seat. He's dehydrated: his lips chapped, his eyes red... Hugh's sees it everywhere in this new existence. The headache he has is probably awful.

He reaches behind the seat and grabs the neck for a bottle of club soda and wrangles it into the Mark's lap while keeping the other hand on the wheel.

"Keep your eyes on the map," Hugh says. "We're looking for Cherry Park Road. Have you found it yet?"

The Mark scrabbles his fingers over the cap of the club soda and tips the bottle back, swallowing greedily. Almost immediately, he chokes, his spittle cascading across the dash and his own lap.

"Easy!"

The Mark hacks. "You don't know how long it's been. Feels like days..."

"Probably has been. You've marched right into the absolute driest part of the country. There was barely any water here *before* the drought." Hugh squints at an upcoming road sign and once he reads it, continues driving on. "Cherry Park Road. Come on."

"You still haven't told me what's going on." Annoyance has ebbed back into the Mark's voice again. "Come on: you said you would explain. Who is Elixir? Why do you think my sister is with them?"

"You told me your sister came out here in search of a clinic," Hugh murmurs. "What do you know about it?"

"Not much," The Mark laments. "Ruby was in therapy for a bit after our mom was diagnosed. She had other problems: you know. She was sensitive."

Hugh frowned. "What does that even mean?"

The Mark takes another sip of the club soda. "I don't know. I guess she just emotional?"

"So, because she wasn't as resilient to this apocalypse as the rest of you, she was automatically broken?" Hugh clicks his tongue. "Load of bollocks, that is."

"Hey, I thought it was helping her. And she never made it seem as if it wasn't. That's why when she heard about this clinic, she took off running to find it. She thought it might help. And I...wasn't much help."

Hugh recognizes the faraway look in the Mark's eyes.

*"Just like you."*

He stares beyond the headlights, trying to ignore Amos in the backseat. "What's the atlas say? Are we going in the right direction at least?"

The Mark holds the beaten-up gazetteer closer to his face, trying to read it in the dim overhead dash lights. "Um...Yeah. Yeah. We're going to want to take a left soon."

Hugh taps on the brakes as the car passes an intersection. "*That* left?"

"Soon. I said 'Soon!'"

Hugh stomps on the gas until he reaches the next intersection and takes the corner hard.

*"Someone's throwing a tantrum,"* Amos grouses.

Silence pervades the car once again but not for long.

"So," The Mark exhales. "Is Elixir the name of the clinic my sister was talking about?" A chill has overtaken his words, one that burns off the frustration Hugh is beginning to feel again.

"Yes. And no. Better to say, they are a part of what used to be the clinic your sister came out here to find. I'm sure that one hasn't been a proper functioning facility since the beginning of the Collapse."

The Mark swallows. "I'm not sure I like the sound of that."

Hugh shakes his head. "You're not going to like what else I have to tell you. But first I need to know where I'm headed. Any other turns?"

"Stay on this. We'll be coming to 3rd and Peterson after five intersections. We'll want to take a right."

"The Park Clinic was just like a lot of other places before the Collapse, touting their expertise of being able to fix people. This one specialized in grief—call it a retreat even. Some place that you could go to reset, get back in touch with yourself. Talk about your feelings."

"It doesn't sound all that bad."

"In theory, it shouldn't have been. The place was run by a Doctor Park Butcher but he preferred people to call him by his first name. And then pretty soon, it became Mr. Park to his clients: this semi-formal charade to make him appear more like your best friend, the kind of person you'd tell all your secrets to."

"A guy with two last names?" The Mark scoffs. "I'd be suspicious from the get-go."

"Rightly so... Is this the turn?"

"Yeah."

They veer to the right.

"You'll want to take the second exit on the roundabout."

The car careens along the circle before progressing straight.

"Mr. Park was said to have a guaranteed method to work through ones grief and have his patients feeling like themselves again in no time." Hugh sighs. "I remember the ads. They stretched from coast to coast. 'Embrace the new you.' Just from the amount of money spent on advertising, I imagined he was making money hand over fist, picking up clients every day. But...then there came the rumors.

"Some woman showed up at a police station in Edna Creek claiming she'd escaped from Park's clinic. She was ranting and raving about waking up on an operating table, about being drugged. Said there were monsters roaming the halls."

The Mark's eyes bug. "What happened to her?"

"The clinic shut down before authorities could look into it. The building was put up for sale, cleared out... Everyone thought she was mad."

"Did you think so?"

Hugh blinks. "Suppose so. But I honestly wasn't focusing on it. It was one of just a dozen batty stories coming out every day, everyone harder to believe than the last."

In truth, Hugh hadn't remembered the event so much as he remembered reading about it as research for his trip to Mal Verdugo. Elixir was a name synonymous with the city: one that was often spoken in hushed tones in bars throughout Nothingland, in the shadows of ruined towns where people still feared the boogeyman showing up to kill them. If it wasn't Hugh or one of his fellow hitmen, then it was an acolyte of Elixir.

The Mark looks back at the map. "Shit. Um... we missed a turn but it's okay! We can take the next left."

Hugh slows down and does so.

"We should be getting close now. We'll hit Cherry Park Road after two lights—Cherry *Park* Road. Ugh, don't tell me—"

"It's a coincidence."

"Are you saying that fuck is here? Mr. Park? That this clinic is the one Ruby wants to—"

"I've told you: it's not a clinic anymore. Since the place shut up shop, it's become kind of an urban myth. There have been rumors that this local group, Elixir, has ties to it though. Namely, the pamphlets they hand out have a familiar tagline." He passes the crumpled paper from his lap over to the Mark. He hears the paper rustling followed by the Mark's breath suddenly getting heavier.

"'Embrace the new you.'"

"Elixir has a reputation. People who are seen with acolytes, like the woman we were chasing, don't tend to come back. I've heard it from many people in lots of different places. Now, we're going to see it for ourselves."

The Mark's face scrunched in fear. "Oh, that sounds like a great idea. 'Oh, no one's ever seen again. Right: let's go do the same thing they did. Should be a fucking riot.'"

Hugh slows the car down and parks on the side of the road before they reach the corner. They get out and proceed to the opposite side of the road, looking out on the intersection of Cherry Park Road and Duchovny Ave.

"We'll walk the rest of the way. A car out here might be too suspicious." Hugh sets out down the sidewalk, the Mark behind him.

ANGER

# MONTHS AGO

There were fires. They swept the land, ate up what remained of dry forests and wide-open fields. In a way, Hugh was glad that Amos hadn't been around to see them. Not that he'd have understood in his declining health anyway. But his love had always feared it, like some people feared the dark or deep water.

The fires still burned in Kohaltine. It was a windy city, so naturally they were always fueled. It would cut down the alleys, down the streets, down the gutters and high above in the skyscrapers. There was no escaping it. Like there was no escaping the judgement he brought to his next mark.

Hugh found him in the local park, his set-up beneath the bridge that led toward one of the city's most notable landmarks, the Fountain of Scorpio. He could see it glimmering dimly in the distance. Trees smoldered; the thick smoke carried by the gusts. Hugh had scrounged a gasmask from the pawn shop in Nothingland, the kind with the large nozzle fitted on the end, the hoses branching off the sides like elephant ears. His vision was marred, the plastic eye sockets scratched and yellowed with age.

But there was no mistake: the huddled shape surrounded by cardboard and threadbare blankets was *him:* the latest target.

The Old Mark regarded him from the bundles of ragged sweaters and patchwork jackets. "Took you long enough," he croaked.

Hugh didn't say anything.

"Cat got your tongue?"

Silence, save for the trees burning.

"You're the Maestro then? I heard about you. Word travels like the fire if you hadn't already wondered."

"*I wonder what they say about you,*" Amos whispered in his ear.

Hugh cleared his throat.

"Curious, aren't you?" The Old Mark spoke through the folds of his sweaters. "Or maybe not. You don't seem like the type who gives a hoot what people say about him."

"What did you do with all the money?" Hugh finally asked.

"What's it look like I did with it?" the Old Mark bit.

"Well, it's certainly not here, is it?"

"I donated it where I could. Shelters, relief efforts, hospitals… It went just as quick as it came." The Old Mark shrugged. "It helped for a while. My satisfaction came taking it from that fucking asshole, Steele, and actually doing something good with it."

"*Hmm.*" Amos hummed. "*Someone decent for a change.*"

Hugh ignored him. "Even knowing he would come after you for not repaying him?"

"Who gives a rat's ass what happens to me?" The Old Mark chuckled. "Like I said: I did some good. I got my revenge."

The word sparked in Hugh's ears. "Come again?"

"I knew him back from Hollywood. We did a film. I can still picture it's title screen: *The Devil's Gait.* Critics hated me. Loved him. Somehow."

Hugh recognized the name on his file now. Didn't remember if he'd seen this movie or really any of the mark's films. Amos had once said he looked like someone had—

"*—rolled a boulder onto his forehead and left it there for six hours.*" Amos grinned in his head.

"You did this because he got reviewed better?"

"No." The Old Mark lifted his head for the first time to face him. Hugh now saw the opaqueness of the man's eyes, how the skin was reddened and the flesh scarred around them. "He was awful to people then just as he is now. Mistreated the crew behind set. Mistreated his fellow actors. It didn't matter. People still loved him.

"Way I saw it: he got off on proving people were horrible at their core. He gave money out just to see how they'd abuse it. The only way to beat that was to use his money for a positive cause. So, I turned around and gave it to every organization I could trying to keep this world together. That fucknut can eat my dick."

The Old Mark wriggled out from his blankets and opened his arms with a sigh. "You're just doing your job. Get on with it then."

Hugh inhaled through the mask. "It's not going to be quick."

"I didn't expect it would be."

Trash skittered along the cement path on the other side of the tunnel. In the background, the crackling of fire breaking down the trees was like static. He wanted to believe they were alone, enough to tell the Old Mark that what he'd done was noble. But he couldn't shake the feeling…

Steele was always watching.

Hugh reached out his hand and forced his blood to sing. Sometimes, it had a cadence like music that disturbed him, that brought him back too close to the memories of before and when it did, he had to make it more discordant, shriller, more dizzying so that it felt like he wasn't sure what was up or down because all that filled him was the sound.

He'd never seen another human being on fire before. But the man ruptured into it like dry leaves to a spark, the blankets and jackets feeding the inferno. The man's long hair and beard flared immediately, the hairs curling and sparking as his face burned red like candle wax, as his lips curled and blackened. The scream burrowed into Hugh like worms into soft dirt.

Wheezing through the mask, Hugh turned and left the flaming park, trying to make the goosebumps disappear.


His car ran out of gas on the way back. The place was familiar, an echo of himself already there. And just beyond the next hill lay that retro gas station, the colored walls screaming out against the sand and the endless sky. It was afternoon this time, the sun's heat blistering. He used his suit jacket for cover, though the going was longer. The cut had healed with herbs and words ago, but the limp and a scar remained, a ghost of the trauma he'd endured.

Step by step, he hefted the empty jerry can. He looked back over his shoulder. He couldn't leave the car for too long.

By the time he reached the gas station, the wound in his thigh stung.

There was no music playing: only the rhythmic ratcheting of a socket wrench. This time, the mechanic caught sight of him as soon as he appeared in the doorway. It took him a moment longer before he said, "Oh, hey! Fuck-If-I-Care, right?"

Hugh exhaled, trying to let his breath catch up. Finally, he spoke. "Petrol."

"See you're still as friendly as ever." The Mechanic rolled his eyes and went back to tinkering.

Hugh regarded the old sandblasted pump baking in the heat. He draped the jacket over his head, knowing that would leave his arms and hands unprotected.

As he started to step back out of the garage, the Mechanic cleared his throat. "I told you this time it wasn't going to be free."

Hugh remained where he was. "I have nothing to give you." It was a lie. He could offer him one of his cards, the smallest token of appreciation he could afford to anyone who helped him out. It was something the Witch hadn't noticed yet in her routine observations of him and if she had, she allowed it for whatever reason.

The Mechanic's mustache twitched. His gaze swept to the office for a moment before returning to Hugh. "Write something."

Hugh frowned. "What?"

"For my payment, I would like you to write something. It can be anything. But it has to be at least a page long. Once it's done, I'll turn on the pump for you."

Bugger this. He could kill the Mechanic, turn on the pump himself. But…this shop was enormous and filled with junk. The stench of oil and grease made his senses cloudy. He wasn't sure he could find whatever switch or control box or key activated it and he might spend hours looking for it.

More importantly, he couldn't leave the car for that long.

Huffing, he sidestepped the Mechanic, sat in the dingy office chair and shook the mouse on the trackpad to bring the screen to life. An empty space awaited, cursor blinking.

It felt like a million years had passed since he'd used a computer. He wasn't even sure when the last time had been. Of course they were still around, but he hadn't touched one since…

He took a shuddering breath.

Since…

AMOS STARED AT THE BLACK SCREEN. Hugh knew if he went over and turned it on for him, he'd complain. He'd get mad. But he was just sitting there and the lines in his face were getting deeper with every passing second.

It would be worse if he asked. But he couldn't stop himself from saying, "Is it giving you trouble?"

Amos snapped out of his daze, looked over his shoulder. "Huh?"

"Just let me know if I can…you know." Hugh couldn't look in Amos's direction as he casually said the words.

"No…" Hesitant yet firm. "I'll figure it out."

Another five minutes went by. He'd finished making their sandwiches for lunch, even cut the crust off Ella's for her. The computer was still off.

"Come have some lunch," he called. "That can wait a bit longer."

Amos erupted. He'd said...

He'd said...

He couldn't remember.

He couldn't remember what Amos had said. What he did.

"Better get writing, Tolstoy."

The garage. The office. The computer.

Hugh blinked and ire flickered to life like an old bulb in his brain. He typed a single word. Enter.

Single word. Enter.

Single word. Enter.

All the way until the bottom of the page.

He stood up, letting the chair roll back into the bookshelf and walked out.

The Mechanic looked at him warily. "That was fast."

"Petrol." Hugh nodded to the pump. "Turn it on."

"What did you write?"

"It doesn't matter, remember?"

Hugh watched him lean in and glance at the monitor before returning his sights to him. "I said that." He disappeared around the corner and even as Hugh tried to move to see where this precious switch was, he couldn't do it in time before the Mechanic had already turned around. "All yours, Fiic."

Hugh pumped his gas, the sun blazing into him as the jerry can steadily filled. The walk back to the car was even longer, his thigh burning almost instantly as he began moving. Filling the car took forever. He studied the newspaper-covered windows in the backseat as the gasoline glugged into the tank, until the jerry can was empty. He tucked it in the boot and returned to the driver's seat.

Humidity welcomed him as he buckled the seatbelt, turned the key, and drove back to Nothingland.

Fuck

Fuck

Fuck

FUck

FUCK

FUCK

fUCK

Fuck

FucK

fuck

fuck

fuck

fuck

FuK

fuck

FUCK

FUCK

FUCK

FUCK

FUCK

# MAL VERDUGO

"WHAT IF THIS PLACE ISN'T AS BAD AS PEOPLE THINK IT IS?" the Mark asks as they amble down the sidewalk of Cherry Park Lane. The wind has picked up and roils around them angrily, bits of sand scraping their skin.

Ahead of them stands a cavalcade of office buildings, cold and presumably empty, their windows black. These places are locked up tight; the rich assholes who vacated them likely secured each one with the most impressive tech they could. It was hard to imagine a world where in spite of people dying in the streets and praying for refuge, electric locks still fastened bulletproof glass doors, security systems remained active, and motion sensors tracked the tiniest movements, even that of spiders and mice.

To Hugh, they feel more than just liminal, as if whole empty universes exist inside of them, foreign from the hell happening outside. The prospect of their emptiness horrifies him. To exist apart from the suffering... It seems monstrous. Ignorant. Callous.

"What if it's just all sunshine and puppies with this Elixir group?" the Mark continues, clearly unaware of Hugh's observations. "Closed off from the rest of the world. That could happen, right?"

Hugh glares at him. "How likely does that sound?"

"I don't care how likely it sounds. I just want Ruby to be okay. If this place is really helping her, who am I to stand in the way?"

Stopping, Hugh faces the Mark. "You didn't come all the way out here because you thought she was okay. You didn't ask a bunch of strangers to help you find her because you thought she was okay. We're not here now because you think she's okay. Placating yourself is only going to make the reality of what's happening to her hit harder."

The hope evaporates from his face.

*"Jesus, Hugh,"* Amos scolds from the shadows. Hugh can barely see the reflection of a nearby streetlamp on his glasses.

He takes a deep breath through his nose. "There may still be time to save her. Come on."

They continue walking.

At the corner of Resina Avenue and Cherry Park Road is a bus shelter with two people crowded on the bench inside it. One wears two winter jackets, the outer most one purple and puffy, a scrunched winter cap pulled down over their head, hands wrapped in thin gauze. The other wears almost nothing: the turquoise flannel draping from one bony shoulder, his face sharp and eyes sunken.

Hugh puts a hand up to stop the Mark and they scuttle into the shadows to watch.

"Every bus shelter I've seen in this city is full of people's belongings or turned into a camp. Not this one?" the Mark says.

"Clearly, it's got a reputation," Hugh answers.

"It's a meet-up spot," the younger adds.

The beam of headlights shines through the dark moments before a blue van turns the corner, the kind Hugh remembers seeing parked at the agriculture store near home. Someone was always transporting equipment around with it, the outsides battered and dented, paint-chipped and dulled. It stops in front of the shelter, blocking their view of the occupants.

"I can't see what's happening," the Mark says.

Hugh waves for him to follow as they scuttle in shadow back towards the car to a better angle. As they move, they hear the sound of a backdoor sliding open followed by the rustling of people moving. The people on the bench were getting in.

They were going to miss it. Hugh berated himself mentally, realizing he should have stayed with the car from the beginning. *Of course it's a pick-up spot. Of course it is.* Elixir would never be so bold as to put the location of their "clinic" on those pamphlets for everyone to see.

*"Pay attention, love."*

He doesn't realize he was now alone, the kid half-running across the road to get to the bus stop. "Hey, wait!" The Mark's voice comes out high and wobbly. "Don't leave without me!"

"Shit." Hugh holds his breath, legs moving faster toward the stolen Mercedes. "Shit, shit, shit, shit."

What the hell was he doing? He was going to get himself killed!

*"Don't you see?"* Amos says, his voice coming from every shadowed corner that Hugh passes. *"He doesn't care. He's going to find his sister with or without you."*

The Mark has vanished around the backside of the van. He can hear a little bit of conversing but nothing definite. Moments later, the van door closes.

Hugh turns the corner and runs to the Mercedes, the old door creaking as he throws himself inside. His hands shake as the keys jangle in them. "Blast it. Blast it!"

Amos's hand folds over his. *"You can just let the van leave, you know."*

Hugh looks up into his eyes and gasps.

The face is one he recognizes but only for a moment. A day he wishes he could forget. A day he wishes would wash away like soap through warm water.

*"You know he won't come back. You know they'll do to him exactly what Steele wants. The hardest part. And all you'll have to do is pull the trigger."*

Hugh snorts, stabs the key into the ignition, brings the car to life. He hardens his jaw. "I still have to find out where they're taking him."

The van pulls a U-turn once it's out on the street and heads back in the direction it came from. Headlights out and staying back a good distance, Hugh follows.

# BEFORE

"No."

Such an absolute word. Amos didn't say it often but when he did, he meant it.

"What do you mean, 'no?'" Hugh practically stammered. He sat in the worn-in armchair across from Amos and leaned in. "It's not dangerous—really—it's not. I've read all the books, and it's full-proof. Well, not *full-proof* but close. And that's closer than we've gotten so far."

Amos's eyebrows knit together. "I don't want you to do that for me."

"Well, I'm sorry, but I have to." Hugh shook his head. "Nothing else has worked. This is all we have left to try."

Amos sighed. "I don't want you to waste any more time trying to fix something that can't be fixed. If my memory is going, I want to spend as much time as I can with the two of you before I lose...everything."

Hugh fought the urge to clench his teeth. "Amos, I wouldn't be doing anything that other witches haven't done. Blood magic has been practiced for thousands of years. Some covens *still* practice it. It's the only way."

Amos blinked. "Don't do that. Don't make it seem like it's all that or nothing. That's not fair. I've told you I don't want it and that's my decision."

"So, you'd rather not try?" Hugh's words hissed out of his throat like air escaping through the tiniest crack. "You'd rather accept the inevitable? Accept the fact that your life will be cut short and you'll forget me...Ella..."

With each word, he saw tears form in Amos's eyes.

"The Amos I fell in love with wouldn't give up. He's a fighter. He's stubborn. He'd try anything." Because *that* was the Amos he'd always known: the junior professor at the college where Hugh had visited with his university's orchestra. The academic who fought back against the administration and won when they tried to fire him because of his sexual preferences. The husband who had defended him when the town shunned Hugh at their first farmer's market. The father who could always engage their over-tired and obstinate daughter with a beautifully spun bedtime story and have her asleep in no time.

But this shell of Amos made Hugh sick. Made him angry. Made him want to curse spirits whose names he hadn't recited since the day he initiated his first spell.

Amos had cracked his crooked smile. He took off his glasses and rubbed at the lenses with the sleeve of his shirt. "I'm tired, Hugh."

The words felt like poison. He was all at once caught off guard by the sincerity of his partner's words and the exhaustion that carried on them.

"We have spent months trying tonics, creams, potions, teas and various other herbal remedies and every attempt has led to the same thing: nothing is going to stop this. I don't want to spend any more days throwing up from the side-effects of a spell. I don't want to have to wear sunglasses indoors, or avoid eating anything but dandelion roots and potatoes for a week. I just want to..." The smile withered. "To be with you and Ella."

Hugh swallowed. It hurt to breathe, the feeling like fire soaring in his chest. He asked, "What's the worst you think would happen? Can't we try one more time?"

Amos reached over and grabbed his hands between his own. They felt cold. "No. Because then the Hugh *I* fell in love with would be gone."

# MONTHS AGO

"YOU'RE LATE."

Hugh braced himself for the pain, his entire body stiffening as he stepped further into Steele's sanctum. The firelight was the only color in an otherwise black room full of glossy surfaces. And then came his eyes out of the dark like two blue marbles along with the rest of him.

Hugh waited.

"Liked what you did in Kohaltine." Steele chewed on something, the crunches soft. "Lit him up like a stick of dynamite."

"Everything else was on fire," Hugh murmured. "It felt thematic."

A look crossed Steele's face and while Hugh wasn't sure exactly what it was at the moment, he was sure that it was an emotion very unfit for the man he'd come to know over these long years. Disappointment, perhaps? Or…loss. It didn't belong whatever it was.

"Your new marks are on the desk," Steele said, and reached into his pocket for—Hugh squinted—almonds. Their bitter sweetness perfumed the air around him.

Marks. This was new. "As in more than one?"

"This is a package deal," Steele answered. *Crunch, crunch.* "Siblings.

They both need to go. Don't care which one goes first." The clatter of more almonds against teeth. *Crunch.* "Maybe something like you did for my old co-star, huh?"

THE WITCH WAITED FOR HIM outside the Tower. He wouldn't have seen her if he couldn't detect her aura. It gleamed like vanilla starlight against the night.

"That leg still fucking with you?" she asked.

"No." He couldn't tell her the truth. She'd use it against him at some point. It's not as if she cared.

"I can take a look at it. Did the same for the Neck-Breaker when Steele took his tongue."

That had been a day. A day he hadn't been the focus of his bosses ire for once. He'd had to watch though. The tongue had waggled a little like a discarded tentacle on the ground in all that blood.

"I don't need it," he answered and kept walking.

"Suppose you could also try the Garden of Delights?" The way she said it made it seem as if she wasn't sure. But he knew that was deliberate.

A warning. She knew he'd been there. It felt too nice. It felt like she was trying to get him to let his guard down. And that only meant one thing: she'd be following him even closer on this next kills. These marks were important. Maybe even more so than the woman in Axy Gable.

He said nothing as he left. He needed coffee. He needed sleep.

THE TYPEWRITER CALLED to Hugh in the small room. Hours had passed in the darkness as he flipped from side to side. Until he pushed himself up from the creaking thin mattress and turned on the lights once more.

He scraped out the chair in front of the desk and sat.

And stared.

He thought of Amos sitting in front of the black computer screen and his gut turned sour.

~~Dear Amos~~

No. He just couldn't.

~~Dear Ella~~

Her deep brown eyes. She'd had Amos's eyes.

~~Ella, my darl~~
No.
He shut off the lights and returned to the cot.
Minutes passed.
He turned the light back on. He sat in the chair.

There are sutures holding me together
that I don't want to pull out.

I can't.

They're all I have left of you.

# MAL VERDUGO

The van takes corners like it's being piloted by a child playing with a toy. The driver careens over the yellow line, zigzagging but slowly. Are they drunk? On drugs? Hugh is sure the van will crash before it ever gets to its destination.

In spite of its driver's disastrous handling, the van remains on the road. After fifteen minutes of following it along its bizarre course, Hugh lets out his breath as it approaches a chain link gate at the entrance to an old factory.

Someone gets out from the passenger side and opens the gate. Their body is shielded by a large poncho, the kind that used to protect from rain back when they had rain. They yank the gates wide open and wait for the van to drive through. Once inside, they follow it on foot to an old docking bay where the van parks crookedly.

Groping for the binoculars in the glove box, Hugh peers through them at the van. The driver gets out. He isn't sure if it's his hands shaking, making the binoculars unsteady but both the gatekeeper and the driver's movements seem strange to him, jerky almost. The back door to the van slides open and the three passengers, the Mark included, get out. He doesn't appear harmed but that familiar expression of bewilderment is still plastered on his face.

The passengers follow the one in the poncho up a small set of stairs to the dock and through one of the doors there, the driver bringing up the rear. Just as he turns to enter, Hugh sees his face. A hot bolt of shock hits his insides. He blinks. In that split second, he was sure there was something very wrong with that man's mouth. Like it was open much wider than any mouth should be, more than a human jaw *can* open...

*Get a move on, you old fool,* he tells himself. *It's the darkness. It's your old eyes. Get in there.*

Hugh gets out of the Mercedes. A low rumble emanates from beyond the buildings that feels like thunder, but he knows is likely a dust storm. The air tastes like a battery on his tongue getting ever stronger as the moments pass. He needs to get inside.

He wanders the sidewalk out front like a stray dog, following the chain link fence, regarding the barbed wire at the top and the pieces of stray fabric that flap in the growing gusts. At the fence post near the bottom corner, the metal wire has been pried away from the edge, bent and twisted.

*"Someone's escape perhaps?"* Amos questions, his voice like particles of sand carried on the air.

Hugh hooks his fingers in the diamonds and pulls, pries, digs his heels in until he's yanked it further away, made a larger opening for himself to slip through.

He almost expects alarms to begin blaring once he sets his foot on the dirt lot. Attack dogs to be unleashed. Armed guards to descend from unseen perches. The only sound is the rustle of the storm beyond the towers. He climbs the landing to the dock and tries one of the closest doors. It shouldn't open but it does. No one is guarding it? No locks on the doors?

Perhaps it's as the Mark suggested: people were there of their own free will. They can leave or come as they want and the barren illusion outside and all of the secrecy is to keep those who would start trouble away.

But...

That fence was pried open from the *inside*.

Hugh enters the unlocked door.

# BEFORE

Dread. It lanced through every blood vessel, seeped out of every pore. Hugh knew the other patients and families watching him could feel his desperation as if it were painted thick on him and drying...slowly.

The nurse was kind enough, talking animatedly, flourishing her hands and fingers with excitement. He kept his eyes on her peach-colored nails to make it seem as if he was paying attention. He was...but not only to her.

He longed to hold Amos's hand. They'd barely said a word to one another in the car on the way over, and even though the drive had only been a half an hour, it felt like years had gone by with every second.

Thankfully, Ella didn't seem aware of the tension, or at least, she didn't appear so. Her attention was locked on the new plastic fox figurine that Amos had bought for her at the store in town. She talked to it, made it leap and run along the wall as they walked down the corridor to the elevator. At one point, she tried to make it climb the side of Amos's suitcase and he'd had to tell her no.

In spite of how little Amos had packed, the wheeled luggage felt like dragging a cartload of bricks. Amos hadn't let him help with the packing. What if he forgot some of his favorite books? Favorite clothes? That photo he'd framed of the three of them so that he wouldn't forget...

The elevator door opened and the nurse guided them in, still talking. Still going over the daily schedules.

"Tuesdays, after breakfast, we have art time! Lots of different workshops to be chosen. Painting, sculpture, performance... Your husband told us you enjoy writing poetry. We have a number of prompts you can choose from for inspiration!"

He ought to have paid attention. Amos certainly was. He was locked in, a pleasant smile on his face the whole time as she spoke. He nodded and said things like "Really?" and "Is that so?" At least he was taking this transition well. It had been his idea. Of course *he* was taking it well.

The elevator opened into a sunlit hallway, just as white as the one they'd walked downstairs. The cream carpet squished under their shoes as they followed the nurse to a room near the end of the hall. The door was wide open and inside lay what Amos would have once referred to as a hotel room for the aesthetically bland. An open room with a bed to the left of the door, a small seating area on their left that looked out over a field of wildflowers, and a bathroom on the right. The walls were bereft of any art: just painfully green walls, the color of sea glass.

God, this was horrible. So plain. So cold. Hugh's gaze bounced back and forth from wall to wall. How could Amos have preferred *this* to staying at home? How could he have chosen this over trying Hugh's idea?

"You'll be staying in the Choate Room!" The nurse exclaimed. "This one offers gorgeous views of—"

"I'm sorry," Amos interrupted her, still that polite smile plastered on his face. "I'd love to learn more but I'm feeling a bit tired. Would you mind if I took a few minutes with my family?"

Panic percolated in Hugh's brain. Fuck. Maybe he'd changed his mind?

The nurse's grin retracted into a demure smile. "Of course. I'll be right outside." She slipped through the door like a cat and closed it behind her.

Ella was already letting her toy fox roam across the stiff-looking furniture in the seating area, murmuring to it as she galloped it along.

"Crikey, I wasn't sure she was ever going to stop talking," Amos said under his breath to Hugh. A bit of old Amos showing himself. Hugh almost choked on his laugh.

"Didn't you want to learn more about the gorgeous views?" he forced himself to joke.

"If I did, I thought you might keel over. You do realize you're practically the same color as the walls, don't you?"

Hugh swallowed.

Amos frowned at him. "I know this is going to be hard. But this way, you don't have to stop what you're doing to take care of me. And hell...maybe I can..." His voice faded.

Hugh wanted to say what he was thinking. Wither away in peace. Everyone knew that facilities like this never solved dementia. They were where the inevitable decline of the human brain reigned. They were the places for those who were giving up on their loved ones, whether it was because of financial woes, time management issues, emotional or physical fatigue...

Amos took hold of Hugh's arms suddenly, rubbing his palms up and down them. "It's okay, you know. I want this."

Hugh's face crunched. "Is it okay?" He shook his head. "I don't think so."

"Hugh..." He let his hands drop. "It's my choice. I choose this. I choose for you and Ella to keep on living. I love you too much for either of you to have to give up anything for me. Not your heart. Not her innocence. You understand?"

Hugh's lip trembled as he looked over his partner's shoulder to make sure that Ella couldn't hear. "So, you're the only one who can make a sacrifice, Amos? Is that it?"

"We've already been over this."

"It's not too late." Hugh tightened his grip on the handle of Amos's suitcase. "We can still go home. We can still—"

"Curse your heart by selling your soul in a blood magic ritual?" Amos said it about as casually as one would ask to pass the salt at the dinner table. "No, Hugh. Just no."

The door opened again before he could do the same with his mouth and in stepped a strapping man, maybe in his late forties by the look of him. A dark beard forested his chin and his hair had been pushed back with some sort of pomade that smelled like lime. He introduced himself as the head of the clinic: Doctor Mann. When they shook hands, Hugh's felt swallowed inside the doctor's cavernous grip.

"We'll take good care of him," Mann assured. "Good care."

Good care, indeed.

# MAL VERDUGO

Hugh has certain images in mind when he steps through the factory door. A warehouse inside full of rusted conveyer belts, chains hanging from the ceiling with bodies bundled in plastic, metal staircases and pulley systems and perhaps some greenish flickering lights to cast a sickening pall over the place, a few that wouldn't even come on.

But that's not what he sees.

It's a vacant waiting room. Not unlike the one he found himself in at a hospital they visited once, the one where they discovered Amos's condition. They were out-of-state visiting one of Amos's friends from the college. It was late at night, the waiting room practically empty save for some middle-aged ladies, one of whom was holding her stomach and moaning.

A bruise had formed on Amos's face. He'd fallen so suddenly it caught them both off guard. Hugh hadn't even seen it happen until he heard glass shatter and saw his husband land at the bottom of the stairs up to their hotel room, the bottle of wine leaking down through the open treads in the stairwell.

"They're going to think I hit you," Hugh had murmured.

Amos chuckled as he responded. "Well, that's ridiculous. I happen to know your aim is atrocious. All those times we played in that softball league?"

Someone clears their throat and it makes Hugh swivel around faster than he's ready for. In the swirl of white, he takes in a glass window off to the side of the small room and a dark silhouette standing inside of it. Hugh holds his hand at the ready as he weaves around the line of uncomfortable-looking plastic chairs, his blood simmering.

In the dimness of the small glass window, a face stares out at him, unmoving. A mannequin. Someone has applied a rubber mask to it, the kind he used to see in stores around Halloween, always grotesque and strange and the facial features exaggerated. This one makes his insides churn. It is almost waxy, the skin pierced and stretched into a wide mouth, with a smudge of pink makeup around the cheeks and smeared on the lips... Someone has done their damndest to make it look real...

It twitches.

Then it turns.

*Fuck!* Hugh staggers back, hand up, nerves jangling.

"Are you itching to taaaalk?" it says, pivoting its head. "Are you burdened by the dark?"

Forcing air into his lungs, Hugh takes a step forward. An animatronic. He can see the bits of steel in its mouth, hear something clunking and ticking. The fuzz of the recording that's playing is almost too loud but at least it makes him feel sane.

"Welcome to Elixir. " It trills. "Tell us your r-ready and we'll open our doors for you. You can become the new y-you in no time! Just tell us when you're re-ready."

The recording clicks off. The creature stills.

Hugh watches it a moment, at the way its gray eyes stare at him almost expectantly.

*"Well..."* Amos says. *"I think it's waiting for you to say something."*

"You've got to be fucking joking," he answers.

*"I don't know."* Amos glides in from behind him, tilting his head a little at the thing behind the glass. *"It feels like it's listening."*

"I'm not speaking to that thing."

*"Then I guess you're not getting inside."*

Grinding his teeth, Hugh eyes the door to his right. It looks solid and there's a numbered keypad above the door handle. Even though he knows it won't budge, he still tries it. Firmly locked.

He returns to the thing at the window and clears his throat, glaring at Amos for only a moment before saying, "I'm ready."

The animatronic doesn't move.

*"Louder,"* Amos prompts.

"I'm ready!"

"Wonderful!" the voice cheers and the sudden explosion of movement from the creature makes him jolt. "All you need to walk through that door is to talk. Just talk. Welcome home. We can't wait to meet the new you!"

Returning to the door, he tries it again. Still locked.

"Hey, Bit's and Bolts, the door isn't opening," he yells back at the creature.

It doesn't answer him, locked in its dead-eye stupor once more.

The keypad. It isn't numbers. It's letters.

Talk.

Just TALK.

Hugh types in each letter and the lock thumps open.

Amos frowns. *"Simple."*

"I doubt the rest of this place will be as such." Hugh twists the knob and pushes through. A corridor stretches ahead of him. The walls have been plastered, wooden bulkheads made to appear warm and antique. This doesn't feel like being inside a factory, more like stepping into a home like the one he grew up in back in England. There is even an Oriental rug laid out on the varnished wide-boarded floor.

The smell of vanilla and something else reaches out to draw him further inside. And once he identifies it, it sends a thread of fear down his back. It smells like oil.

In the distance, a rhythmic banging calls to him followed by shouts.

No.

*Screams.*

# MAL VERDUGO

"**I** KNEW THIS PLACE WAS TOO GOOD TO BE TRUE," Hugh says to himself as he walks the corridor. The pounding continues. The screaming. The echoes feel like splinters under his fingernails with every step. "I told you, didn't I? But you and the Mark just have to keep foisting the idea of happy puppies onto me. Well, I'm telling you now, if there are puppies here, they're blood-thirsty, ravenous puppies."

*"You can't blame the boy for wanting to think on the bright-side."* Amos answers from somewhere behind him. *"I'm honestly indifferent."*

"Of course you are."

"Hey, I didn't put you here. You chose this."

There's offense in that statement and it nearly spins Hugh back around. But he focuses on the banging and turns at the end of the hall. A set of stairs awaits him, each tread covered by a decorative bit of green carpet. But it's the state of the hall that pulls at his attention. Bits of trash. Dust. Stains on the carpet. As though turning the corner was where the effort to disguise this place died.

Hugh climbs the stairs, taking each one softly and keeping his eyes ever upward. The next level loses any and all of the warmth it had below. The rug lining the hall is dingy, holes worn through it as though scuffed by dragging feet. The doors that line this corridor look like wood but as soon as he lays a hand on one, he realizes it's been painted to appear that way. They are steel, with small barred windows to look inside. He can feel the aura of a heart pulsing behind the door but when he looks in, he sees nothing in the dim space.

It's almost impossible to concentrate through the reverberating banging happening from down the hall. "Let me the fuck out of here! Hey!"

The Mark.

Hugh scans the doors: eight in total. The last one is unlike the others, an actual wooden door opened a crack and from inside comes a sound that makes Hugh's skull vibrate: whirring. Like a dentist's office. The high pitch makes his stomach swim like worms are trying to penetrate it. Where there was once screaming there is only the high whirring, the Mark yelling from his cell...

"WE'RE GOING TO NEED TO INCREASE YOUR MONTHLY BILL."

Hugh could hardly hear the other end of the telephone line. The tinnitus in his ears consumed him as panic drowned his thoughts.

"What? What do you mean?"

"You've seen the news. You've seen what's going on out there." Doctor Mann somehow kept his voice irritatingly calm throughout the call, almost like an anesthesiologist administering an injection. "Resources are strained. In order to continue to care for your husband, for all of our patients, we're asking all of our clients to agree to an upcharge to ensure that care remains undisturbed. Otherwise, we may need to release him back into your custody. For his own good."

Hugh's pulse raced. He had seen the news. Every night. On his phone during the day. At his computer. It was non-stop. An onslaught of horrible images. People and wildlife struggling, dying... Borders closing. Wars escalating. Federal aid collapsing. Hospitals overcrowding. Looting. Markets crashing.

Every day. More. More. More.

Hugh knew it was only a matter of time. They lived outside of town, off the grid, on their own land. They could ride it out for a little while. But Amos...

Hugh couldn't pull him out of there now. He was at his breaking point. Money was tight enough as it was. He'd already had to take out a loan to cover the third month's payment to the hospice center. Whatever Amos had had saved up was lost when the stock market crashed. And their insurance... They were now asking for evidence of a marriage certificate before they would renew benefits. For the life of him, Hugh couldn't find it. Amos used to handle all of their paperwork. He'd been searching for three days now.

"Are you there? Hugh?"

He exhaled, pinched his nose. "I'm here."

"If you can't make the payment, I can have Amos packed up and ready to go by this evening. We have lots of potential patients looking for care right now. His space would be ideal for any one of—"

"No! I can do it. I can pay."

"Alright." For the first time in the call, Doctor Mann actually sounded more than neutral. He sounded relieved. "We expect that payment first thing on—"

"HUGH!"

He snaps his eyes open. Between the bars in the window down the hall, he spies the Mark's desperate face. "Get me out of here!" he pleads.

Hugh's impulse is to run to it and get the Mark out, but the ghost of Amos apparates in front of him as though twisted together from the nearby shadows. *"Stop and think. That room at the end of the hall is open. Whoever is inside might hear you."*

Brushing by him, Hugh notes that the doors don't have locks on them, just crude-looking iron bolts. Strange.

From the room, the mechanical whirring grows more intense. It's beginning to sound more like an electric drill now.

Stopping in front of the Mark's door, Hugh puts a finger to his lips. The Mark goes quiet, mouth-parted and breathing loud enough to be mistaken for a stalker on a phone call. As Hugh begins to step away, he starts to say, "What the hell! Don't leave me—"

"Shut it!" Hugh nips before continuing to the door at the end of the hall and cautiously peeking inside.

# BLOOD

# SO MUCH

# BLOOD

Amos.

Amos.

Amos.

Amos.

He's running.

Everything is a blur.

Every room is the same.

Every hall is white.

His body is amorphous, a void.

Amos.

No.

No.

NO.

THIS ROOM IS HELL.

The blood alone is enough to spike Hugh's own, send it cascading through him like lightning.

The first thing he sees is the stretcher, like a dentist's chair arched back beneath an operatory light. The body is bathed in white, stripped naked, splashes of black on the pale skin. Something viscous. He makes himself look away: decorum, fear, and shame scurrying for dominance in his skull.

He makes himself look again.

Clothes are scrunched on the floor nearby, the turquoise flannel torn and blood-soaked.

There is nothing in the young man's eyes but death. Yet they move. Even with the surgeon's hands buried in the innards of his throat. Hugh sees what looks like a dull rubber hose and realizes too late it's an esophogus, limp and dangling over the edge of the man's neck. The sharp ZZZ-ZZZZ of a drill is like water boiling in a tea kettle within Hugh's mind.

The tray nearby is covered in pieces of metal. At first he wonders if it's just drill bits, tools... But there are sprockets.

Bolts.

Springs.

Gears.

Metal strips with holes for screws.

And a yellow squeeze bottle with a long nozzle. The label says TYPE H CLOCK OIL.

Hugh steps back into the hall, hyperventilating, his nerves firing only one message into the hollows of his brain. Get out. Get out now.

# BEFORE

I**T HAD BEEN NEARLY FOUR MONTHS** with Amos gone from the house. Hugh was bereft. Schedules were the only thing that got him through the days any more. He was awake long before dawn, where he could drink his coffee and commune with the darkness. He lit three pillar candles at the dining room table, ground herbs from their garden with a mortar and pestle. Wildflowers. Honey.

He spoke affirmations though they were tinged with promises: promises he could give to whoever or whatever was listening.

"Look after my family. Look after my blood. I will give my beating flesh if you lessen their coils, lessen their suffering, keep them safe."

And he'd prick his finger, allow a few drops of blood to fall into his mixture before he added hot water to it and drank.

Every day, as he taught Ella her lessons, as he did the household chores, as he toiled in the garden, he listened for the phone call. He expected the hospice center to call, to tell him that his payment had been declined, that they were going to toss Amos out like some kind of spoilt milk. He had to be prepared. He had to do what it took to bring Amos back.

Even if he'd said no. Even if Amos had been against blood magic because he thought it was insidious.

Hugh needed absolutes. He wasn't convinced in the western ideologies of religion, in good versus evil. Demons. Angels. There was only safe magic and powerful addictive magic. The latter was blood magic. And Amos had been afraid of it because he'd come from a family of addicts.

Hugh recognized that. He'd understood the deeper underlying fear that Amos had. But *that* Amos was slipping away.

This was their last chance.

Pricking his fingers day in and day out like a diabetic left them sore. Washing the dishes sometimes reduced him to a trembling mess just from the warmth of the water. He wasn't eating as much as he used to, the herbal spell depleting much interest in it. He had to pretend at dinner sometimes that he was enjoying whatever he made for he and Ella and then afterward, he'd spend an hour throwing it all back up.

The only thing he could stomach were sweet things, which he made very seldomly, for lack of ingredients and because sweets felt like celebration. There was nothing to cheer about. Nothing to be happy for. Nothing.

Nothing except for Ella.

She was the single light in the darkness. When things felt hopeless, one look at her face managed to radiate a faint sense of hope through him. She was still here. She was still strong.

And through her, he fought on. He continued with the spell. He drank the potions. He said the words.

Amos was going to get better. They were going to be fine. The world was on fire but everything was going to be fine.

# BARGAINING

# MAL VERDUGO

THE BOLT ON THE MARK'S DOOR SHRIEKS OPEN as Hugh pushes it back. The young man spills out of it in a flurry of shivering limbs. "I thought you were gonna leave me in there! I thought—"

"Nevermind what you thought." Hugh grabs his arm and yanks him toward the staircase at the opposite end of the hall. "We need to leave now."

They're almost to the stairs before the crackle of an intercom spurts from the corners of the hall. A baritone male voice announces, "Nighttime! Free for all! Come on out and introduce yourselves to our new guests."

And the doors in front of them creak open.

Locked in place, Hugh readies his spell of choice, one that will render the subject incapacitated as their own blood boils them from the inside out. It's quick, and completely lethal.

The moment the first person steps out of the cell, Hugh backs down. The woman is clothed in a ratty-looking blue uniform, her hair disheveled and covering her face. She's shuffling, barely staying on her feet it seems and she's crying.

The Mark is already coming around him, going to give her arm support. "Are you o—"

She looks up. The hair slides from her face. "Something's wrooooong with me!" she squeals. The left side of her face is missing skin, the muscle and bone beneath emaciated and dark. "That's what I used to say aaaalllll the tiiiiime. Before I came heeeere."

Hugh snatches the Mark back seconds before she can grab him.

He yelps. "Fucking hell!"

A voice from behind them perks up. "Now I'm the reeeeeeeal meeeee." They spin to see a scrawny man clambering out of his cell. Something is severely wrong with his face, with his jaw and the way it moves.

"Jesus Christ!" The Mark stammers. "Jesus Christ."

Hugh takes aim at the woman in front of them and whispers the dark words, feeling his veins sear to life. But the woman doesn't blink, her thousand-yard stare burning through him, and she staggers closer.

"What the fuck are you doing?" The Mark pushes him. "Go! Go!"

They sidestep her, even as she reaches for them and misses, her body collapsing on the rug along with the sound of a thousand pieces of silverware clattering. They take the stairs two at a time before stumbling into the hallway at the bottom.

The approaching shadows of two figures stretch along the wall in front of them. They can't get back to the waiting room that way.

Hugh shoulders through the closest door to them and they scramble into a room, their footfalls echoing around them in the large space. Hugh squints in the darkness. A cafeteria. A row of several tables with benches attached stretch before them while off to the left, the dark entrance to the kitchen beckons.

"W-w-what the fuck are those things? What were you trying to do to them?" The Mark stammers.

"How the fuck should I know what they are," Hugh grumbles staring at his hands. That spell should have worked. *Had to have.* Every living thing has blood. Needs blood to survive.

Unless...

He thinks about the black ichor he saw splattered across the body in the operating theater upstairs. The bottle of oil on the tray next to it. Unless they aren't *living* anymore... Which means none of his spells will be effective against them. He is powerless here.

"How the hell are we going to get out of here?"

"Unless we want to end up just like them: very carefully." Hugh points toward the kitchen. "This way. Kitchen's often have some kind of emergency back door per fire code." They edge their way across the cafeteria.

The Mark's face screws up in confusion. "You think this place really cares about fire codes?"

"No. But the factory that existed beforehand did. I doubt they built over it. It seems like all the refurbishing that went into this place mostly happened in the front of house anyway."

*"Besides, things that don't live don't need to eat."* Amos adds from somewhere in the shadows.

The doors behind them squeak open.

This time, it's the Mark who is quicker on his feet and pulls Hugh down behind the Bain Marie counter.

The slow clink-clank of moving legs enter.

Hugh eyes the kitchen door only a few feet away but in plain sight of anyone willing to look in that direction. They need to go now.

He puts three fingers up for the Mark: a countdown.

"Whaaaaaat's wrooong?" an eerily high voice calls. "Don't you want to get to know us?"

Hugh drops a finger. Two.

The Mark nods.

One.

And Hugh's leg ignites in pain, the pain of thousands of fire ants crawling and biting inside of it. He collapses back into the counter, his arm banging against a stack of plates. They careen to the floor.

"Oh! Hellooo!"

"Shit!" The Mark grabs his arm, tries to pull him to his feet.

The moment there is weight under that foot, Hugh crashes down again, harder this time. He hisses, "Go! Run!"

The Mark frowns at him, makes to grab him again.

"I said 'GO!'"

"No! Don't gooo!" the creature cries. "Stay with us!"

The Mark groans before climbing to his feet and racing through the kitchen door.

*"Get on your feet, Hugh."* Amos scolds. *"Now!"*

He half-crawls, half-drags his leg across the vinyl floor and through the door into the kitchen. It's cold in there: the darkness crowding in on him as he inspects his surroundings. It's an open space with an island countertop in the center, the borders of the room ringed by countertops, stoves, and deep-fryers. No other exit. No other way out.

"Oh, you're still not re-ready, are you?" the voice calls from outside the door. "We can make you comfortable. Make you re-re-ready." Each time it has to restart the word, it sounds like a needle tracking off-course on a worn vinyl.

Seething, he pokes the scar in his thigh and curses.

That spell. The one he tried upstairs. There is a reason he doesn't do that one anymore. Because of that fucking Dennis look-alike. Because he is the last person Hugh used it on and that fuck had crammed a fork into his leg while doing it. And now, whenever he performs that spell, it has *this* side-effect...

"Mr. Park is going to take special caaaare of you."

It's still there outside the door, waiting.

Mr. Park. The Park Clinic. Just like he had thought.

He searches the counter tops. Even if he can't get out this way, the kitchen is still a perfect place to find a weapon. But as he scans the counters, Hugh realizes there's no signs of typical kitchenware in sight: no knife blocks, no pots or pans, no spatulas, tongs, spoons, ladles...

*"What did I just say out there?"* Amos clicks his tongue. *"They don't eat."*

No, they don't.

There's nothing left to do but hide.

Hugh pulls open the cabinet door beside him and gazes inside. Shelves. He can't fit in there. The pantry door is down the line of cabinets next to him at the very end. He crawls to it, biting his lip to keep from shouting from the pain and quickly clambers inside. It's musty, the space cramped. The only way he can fit is if he stands up and he does so, trying to keep as much weight off the injured leg as he can. It should clear up soon, shouldn't it? He can't remember how long it took him the last time.

"Come out, come ouuuuut..."

Footsteps plod into the room.

Hugh holds his breath. As he tries to focus on anything other than his leg, he realizes that the Mark is still in the room. He has to be. There are no other exits. So where has he hidden himself?

*"You'll need to perform a spell,"* Amos says softly from beside him. *"Carefully."*

A spell while suffering the after effects of the last one is risky. He isn't sure if it will heighten the pain, if he can even concentrate long enough to focus his energy in order to pick up the Mark's aura. But, he is blind if he doesn't, cornered like some sort of lamb awaiting the diseased wolf to strike. He needs eyes.

Conjuring the words into his head, he squeezes his eyes shut harder and speaks.

And the pain answers.

# BEFORE

Hugh used to think these discussion circles were a silly. Surely people didn't actually form a circle with chairs in an empty room. That was something one only saw on the television or in films. But here he was: slumped in a stiff blue plastic chair surrounded by a bunch of people he didn't know all saturated in silence and sadness.

Everything about this group was sad. Their baggy faded clothing, the creases in their faces, the circles beneath their eyes, the unkemptness of their hair... He glanced down at himself. Bollocks. He'd thrown on that sweatshirt from the closet on his way out the door, something...anything to cover up the t-shirt he'd worn for the last few days.

He was becoming one of them.

Well, almost like all of them. One man wore a crisp shirt, his round glasses perched over observant eyes, his blonde hair combed neatly and hands folded in his lap. He looked like a wrestler pretending to be a professor. It was odd and out of place and Hugh didn't like it.

The woman leading the discussion didn't do much moderating, barely keeping the circle on track as they each introduced themselves. They spewed the appropriate amount of trauma in order to win over abject sympathy from their fellow blobs of sorrow.

"My dad doesn't recognize me anymore."

"My mother thought I was her brother."

"My grandfather thinks he's back in the town he grew up in."

Alzheimer's Anonymous or whatever this little group was had been the nurses' idea the last time he stopped by to visit Amos. She had shown him the flyer, designed by someone using a birthday party template in some graphics program. There were far too many colors, confetti, and balloons for the gravitas of this gathering. He wasn't sure why he'd even come.

Maybe just to get out of the house. Maybe just to be away from the things that reminded him of Amos. Reminded him that the world was going to the dogs out there. This room, in a classroom at the local community center, felt stuck in time. His classrooms when he'd still attended university had been exactly like it. He could block it all out in here. Just for a few moments.

He returned his attention to the circle just as the man next to him finished speaking. Blast. It was his turn. The woman at the head of the group shifted slightly in his direction and fixed her exhausted gaze on him. "You're up."

Hugh's eyes shifted around the circle.

They were all staring. Expectantly. Widened red eyes. Pursed lips. As if hearing someone else's trauma would make them feel slightly better about their own. As if they expected him to somehow one-up the previous sharer's heart-rending tale.

"Err..."

A sound leaked out of his mouth and the person to his right exhaled. A sigh of relief. They weren't going to have to go before they were ready.

He stared at his shoes. Was this what was expected of people who grieved? For you to deliver your heartache on a platter, serve it in barely cooked slabs to a bunch of strangers at a very small, very crowded dinner table?

"How about you start with your name?" the Moderator asked delicately and it made him want to curl further into himself.

"My name..." Was he a child she was trying to coax out from their hiding place? "My name is..."

This was pathetic. Why had he ever thought this was better than being at home? It wasn't. It was like air-drying the wet laundry on one long line that the entire neighborhood was using.

He stood up.

The movement caused the rest of the people in the circle to startle, to look at him with admonishment, save for that one puffed up wrestler professor.

"Excuse me," he said and walked out.

The whispers followed him until he pushed out the classroom door. In the hall outside, he took a breath. The fear of home was already beginning to push back into him, like the griminess of his shirt had begun to feel beneath that sweater.

Ella would be asleep by now; the babysitter probably biting her nails and counting the minutes until he returned. He knew the young woman was down on her luck, too. Money was her only motivation for coming so far out of town.

"Hey!"

Hugh half-turned and stiffened seeing one of the other men from the group as he exited the room: the one who didn't belong.

The man strode up to him confidently and though Hugh had always considered himself fairly tall at 6' 2", this man stood over him and outmuscled him easily.

"Kinda like being in a straight-jacket in there, huh?" he said leaning toward him. His voice was low, intimate and his top lip curled up as he talked through his smile. Hugh would have immediately assumed they'd already met, that they were friends with that body language.

Except they weren't.

"Suppose it is," he allowed anyway. "Sorry, can I help you?"

"Just wanted to let you know you're not alone, brother." The man put his hand on Hugh's shoulder, crunched his fingers slightly. "I know they seem dour in there, but every one of those people is feeling exactly how you do."

Hugh's breath felt caught. He cleared his throat and took a small step back, letting the man's hand slide off him. "I appreciate the concern. But I must be going." He started to turn again.

"If these kinds of groups aren't your thing, I offer one-on-one counseling at my office."

When Hugh turned back, the man was holding a business card out to him. It seemed impolite not to take it. Hugh's fingers barely grasped it as he returned his gaze to the man. "You're a counselor?"

"I'm a *doctor*," he rephrased with a chuckle.

Warm.

Casual.

Off.

"You come to these meetings to..." Hugh searched for the word. "Head-hunt?"

The doctor's eyes got round. "Pffft, that seems harsh but I understand the feeling of being blindsided. I know there are people who benefit from a different kind of grief counseling than what's readily available now. And what with everything going to the pits... I just want people to know they've got options."

"How noble of you," Hugh uttered as he handed back the card. "I'd best be going." He took each step firmly, strongly. Every movement he made in the opposite direction away from that wolf in sheep's clothing felt right. It wasn't until he was in the car that he realized he had been holding his breath the whole time and he quickly gaped in the dry, dusty air of the small car.

Amos would have been mad at him for what he'd just done. For causing a scene at his expense.

Hugh gripped the steering wheel, took another deep breath, eyes closed as he tried to imagine what his partner could be doing at that very moment. He was probably asleep. The nurses told him Amos slept a lot.

A knock on his window shattered his peace. He opened his eyes to the doctor grinning in at him from beyond the glass. Hugh's instincts soared, his blood curdling as he scrambled to remember the words to one of the blood magic spells he'd been reading about.

"You forgot your coat," the doctor shouted and held it up for him to see.

Hugh let everything deflate out of him. Rolling down the window, he accepted the heap of wool from the man and gave him a curt nod before driving off. In the rearview mirror, he watched the tall, stout silhouette vanish into the night.

It wasn't until he got home later that he found the card tucked into one of his coat pockets. The name on it was unfamiliar: Mr. Park. There was an address, a phone number, and at the bottom the phrase "Embrace the new you."

# MAL VERDUGO

RAW HUNGRY PAIN seizes him like being snapped up in iron jaws and it takes all of Hugh's will to keep his balance, to keep his knees from buckling beneath him. But when he opens his eyes, colored hazes shift and huddle in the blackness and he knows he's succeeded with the spell.

"Don't you waaaaant to be happy?"

Jaws creak like rusty springs in old beds. The fool can't help it. Hugh isn't sure if she's even aware of it. With every shuddering step, a hinge wrenches wide.

When he has the courage to peek out from the crack in the pantry door, he sees her skin: grey like snails, pasted and slapped back on beneath a flood of stitches and the dull metal glinting in the dimness between her teeth.

Walking and talking. Talking and walking.

Hugh focuses on another color stretched flat beneath a metal shelving unit, almost impossible to see in the darkness. The boy. Not a boy; a man. The Mark. The one he was *supposed* to kill. With a few seconds more, he can hear him. His breath skitters out like wind against fluttering sheets on a line. His aura is a dull pink, thudding against the blue-black of the of the darkness.

The tickle of something on Hugh's leg wrangles his focus, makes him look down for a moment. Blood. It's coursing down his skin, soaking into his sock. The effort to keep the spell going has opened his old wound. He grinds his teeth against the escalating agony.

This is his fault. If he'd just killed the Mark when he'd locked eyes on him, none of this would be happening. If only he'd just done the deed as he was meant to. Even if he hadn't tortured him first, even if he hadn't taken the time to let the Mark's screams fill the void of a neon-filled night in Mal Verdugo… The repercussions from his boss would have been worth it all and he would have survived…

Or maybe Steele would have killed him for good this time.

Better dead than whatever had happened to these poor souls.

"We knoooow this will be hard for you," the springy voice peels through the room like the shriek of metal scraping metal. "It'll all be okay! The new you is cause for celebration."

From the back of the cafeteria: a second voice, higher, more grating like a worn-in armchair. "You don't need to hold on anymore. Holding on hurts. Letting go is better. A breath of freeeeesh air!"

"Fresh air! Doesn't that sound lovely?" A noise akin to that of a busted screen door swinging open. Laughter.

"Just come on out and take my hand—"

"Take her hand—"

"Take her haaaaand." A third one.

Bollocks. Three is too many. Hugh might be able to get the jump on one, wedge something in its snapping jaws, get it to stop talking if only for a few moments so they can make their escape, but three…

They are so fucked.

*"Don't listen to them,"* Amos's voice whispers to him in the dark of the pantry. Hugh nearly jumps, his knee bumping the closet door, the crack widening a bit. He can feel his presence in the small space, the closeness of him, almost smell the soap he used to use back when he was still…

Hugh swallows.

Now isn't the time for that.

"We know where you aaaaare."

Eerily close. Hugh holds his breath.

"We knooooooow…" the screen door calls, as if being stretched open.

He can only see two of them now, the grey of their auras beating darker and darker as his spell fades.

His leg throbs deeper now. His advanced perception ebbs with each pang.

The Mark shouts. The pink glow pulses like a heart as he is yanked out from beneath the rack by his feet.

"Oh, joy! Rhapsody! We found you!"

Hysteria gallops in Hugh's chest.

The Mark is wrenched up from the floor by the scruff of his sweater. He pinwheels his legs uselessly.

Hugh starts to push open the door.

*You'd really give up your life to save someone you're meant to kill?"* Amos asks and it stills Hugh.

Soon enough, both colors fade into the blankness of the wall. He listens as the Mark struggles and calls his name.

*This is how it's supposed to be*, he tells himself, looking down at his bleeding leg. There was never any chance for the Mark, none for his lost sister, none for anyone in this godforsaken world. You are either predator or prey.

Fuck if he cares. That's who he is now.

Fuck if he cares.

"How will you ever heal if you don't talk…"

Hugh's head snaps up.

Eyes leer at him from beyond the crack in the door. Lost eyes. Haunted eyes. Gears clunking away behind them as the mouth ratchets open one click, two clicks, three…

"Talk!" The jaws slam shut, grinding teeth and the metallic bang reverberating through the room. "Talk! Talk!"

The closet door bursts open. Fingernails dig into Hugh's arms and pry him from the darkness. Against all his will, he cries out.

"Yes! Scream like you mean it!" the rust and metal praises. "Scream the old you away!"

# BEFORE

"WHAT'S THAT?"

A cold rectangle of moon slid across their bed. Hugh didn't recognize the shadows; they could come alive at any moment, warm things in the coldness of their room.

"I think...an animal," Amos whispered to him.

Terror gripped him. The scream was of a woman being killed, a woman fighting for her life as someone scrabbled at her with desperate hands. He wanted to bolt up from the bed, to run to Ella's room and make sure she was alright.

Something tossed in the sheets beside him. She was already there, fast asleep. She'd snuck in between them hours before.

Amos reached a hand over the covers to him and set it on Hugh's chest. "It's foxes. I can see them."

Hugh glanced at his partner, who's eyes had greyed over. Amos rarely used his second sight but there in that moment, Hugh knew he was somewhere out amongst the fields rather than in bed next to him, watching whatever happened. "It's a vixen calling for a mate." Moments later, his eyes cleared.

"Christ," Hugh murmured.

"Thoreau used to call the sound 'a vulpine curse,'" Amos remarked under his breath.

"Fitting," Hugh replied. "Feels like being cursed."

The screaming abruptly cut off. Silence flooded in. The goosebumps on Hugh's arms wouldn't fade.

Amos squeezed his hand. "I think it's over."

And Hugh squeezed back. "Is it?"

ANGER

# MONTHS AGO

A RED MOON LIT THE SKY when Hugh returned to the service station in the desert. He wasn't on his way back from a kill. He wasn't out of gas. He didn't pick the date for the celestial significance.

As he got out of the car, the bloody sphere in the dark made him sick to his stomach. There was no hope left. This was a sign of the end, a bloody moon in the night over a barren desert. Far off, a coyote yipped and all the hairs on his arms prickled.

Only the light from a drink cooler glowed inside what was left of the dark convenience store, casting the racks of old food and the counter in a haze of lime green. The bell dinged as he pushed through the shop door and stared at the man sitting behind the counter.

The Mechanic's hands were clasped in front of him as if in prayer. When he opened his eyes, it was to instantly roll them. "You're like a bad cold, Fiic. Just hanging around."

"I need to use your computer."

"Are you serious right now?" He checks his watch. "You drove all the way out here for that. It's almost two a.m."

"The Underground," Hugh said. "I need you to help me find something.

Help me find *someone*."

The Mechanic shook his head and didn't move from his stool. "I told you that the Underground is accessible from anywhere. You didn't need to come all the way out here to—"

"I can't access it where I'm from. I just...can't." Every word that came out of Hugh's mouth was like he was pulling on it, playing tug-of-war with his insides.

The Mechanic's brow furrowed into a pitiful stare.

"Look, if you help me this last time, I'll give you whatever you want."

His brows shot up. "I wouldn't know what to ask for."

"Well, you've got time to think." Hugh sighed. "Please."

Clicking his tongue, the Mechanic got up from the stool. "Well, since you asked so politely." He led Hugh through a door behind the counter that connected with the garage. The ghastly moon glared through the open bay doors, washing the cement floor in its hue. "Hell of a night out there. Strawberry moon, I think."

Strawberries.

STRAWBERRIES.

Picking them in the garden was always a delight. Ella's small fingers cupping them to her as he and Amos delicately set them in her palm.

Washing them in a colander in the sink.

Amos laughing as he sliced them, tossing one back and catching it in his mouth.

Ella grinning, the juice turning her lips red

"Hey."

He blinked.

"Come on, Fiic."

Hugh followed the Mechanic into his office.

"You roll up with all this urgency and then stand there..." The Mechanic muttered as he booted up the computer. The modem chirped and fans whirred to life as the screen lit. He drummed his fingers on the desk. "Anything, eh? That's so... I mean. Obviously you can't get me *anything* I want but..."

"Who says I can't?" Hugh flexed, searching the Mechanic's face.

"...It just seems like a big carrot to dangle for such a little favor." The Mechanic stroked his beard. One eyebrow had worked its way up in question.

"It may seem like a small favor to you, but it means everything to me."

The user password screen popped up. After the Mechanic signed in, the desktop appeared in a flourish. The background was a photo of a beautiful coastal town, warmed by sun and surf.

"Somewhere you went on vacation perhaps?" Hugh pried.

He nodded. "I went there ten years ago. It was the last time I got to go anywhere before the Collapse."

It looked like Ibiza: the rustic white stucco buildings, the turquoise Mediterranean waters, the beaches... Amos had always longed to go. "Well, I doubt it looks the same, but if you want to return there, I could call in a favor."

"I worked my entire life," The Mechanic said softly. "Part of my father's motto: all we have is our work. It gives us purpose. But that vacation..." The Mechanic had a faraway look in his eye. "It was like I finally understood what other people were talking about, about living, even if it cost me to get there... Experiencing life. And yet...here I am at the end of the world...Working."

Hugh blinked. "Me, too."

It was hard to read the Mechanic's face. It had gone blank. Perhaps he would consider it. He negotiated the mouse to an icon on the desktop and double-clicked it. A black window opened on the screen with a white cursor blinking. After he settled into the computer chair, the Mechanic typed in a series of codes: various parentheses, colons, letters and numbers...

"How the hell was I supposed to be able to access this from wherever?"

Hugh growled to himself. "It's like your bloody hacking into the Matrix."

"I assumed that a man who can get whatever anyone wants could probably find someone who knows how to code, at least," the Mechanic joked.

Moments later, a browser sprung into view along with a search bar and a series of links listed beneath it. "Here. Now, what are you looking for?"

Hugh blinked. This was it? The Underground looked so ordinary. But he supposed it had to be so as not to look too suspicious to those who might want to get rid of it.

"Search for Mr. Park. Grief counselling."

The Mechanic stared at him. "Odd thing to be trying to find in this day and age, Fiic."

"Please, just...indulge me."

"Fine." He typed it in. Nothing came up.

"What about Park Clinic? Doctor Park?"

The Mechanic typed. "If you *really* need someone to talk to..."

Nothing. Nothing but posts about parks that people had walked their dogs in, parks where people hoped to meet up in posts from years past. Maybe they had. Maybe they hadn't. Parks in stories from romantic comedies to science fiction. But no Doctor Park and no Park Clinic.

Hugh let out a shuddering breath. The dossier the Witch had given him had said one of his targets was looking for Park's clinic. How else would she have known about it other than from the Underground?

Then, a thought hit him.

"Try: 'Become the new you.'"

Click. Click. Click. "Sounds like some strange bohemian kind of shit but..." He tapped the enter key with his pinky.

Boom.

A result.

One post shared multiple times throughout the message board. When the Mechanic clicked on it, its brief message drove a sense of resolve back into Hugh's chest. "There it is."

The Mechanic nodded. "I've seen this around. Same guy always posts it, this MPinMV."

"Can we bring up a profile? Find out where it's being sent from?"

The Mechanic gritted his teeth. "People stay anonymous on here for a reason, but..." He pressed a few keys on the board and another smaller window popped up. He typed into it furiously. "Sometimes people are sloppy."

"How did you get in to doing this?" Hugh asked him. "I mean, you weren't just fixing up automobiles every day in the middle of nowhere because you wanted to, right?"

"Everyone has an origin story, my friend," the Mechanic droned as he typed. "But...we hardly know one another and that feels like a fifth date kind of thing."

A chime sound from the computer pulled both of their attentions back to the screen. "The IP Address comes from Mal Verdugo. Suppose you're looking for whoever MP is in MV... Mal Verdugo."

"MP..." Hugh grumbled. "Mr. Park."

"He wasn't really trying to hide it. Almost like he wants to be found." The Mechanic cocked his head. "Which I suppose is on brand for the message they keep posting. Almost like an advertisement or—"

Hugh didn't let him finish the sentence. He placed his hands on the Mechanic's shoulders, uttered a string of words that tasted like mildew in his mouth. They slowly burned into ash on his tongue.

The Mechanic jolted, his entire body rigid as the energy cascaded through his brain, short-circuiting, fizzling, shutting down. Hugh imagined the wild images racing through his head in no particular order: past experiences, moments in time, good and bad and in between. Pain and pleasure and anger and despair. Perhaps he'd light on those moments in Ibiza for a few seconds before his brain cooked and the blood coursed out of his ears and his eyes like dark rivers.

It only took about ten seconds or so, and when he was done, the Mechanic's body slumped down into the computer chair like an empty suit.

Sighing, Hugh closed the dead man's eyes, walked to the garage and grabbed a wrench from the tool box next to one of the cars. He swung it into the modem, crunching and smashing until bits of hardware flew and the monitor went black.

He took the picture for evidence of the kill and sent it.

Now. To Mal Verdugo.

# MAL VERDUGO

A WHITE HOT CONE OF PAIN encircles Hugh as he is thrown from the kitchen pantry. He's sure he blacks out—or whites out—and is overcome by the feeling of spring grass tickling the back of his neck. The white turns to an azure sky full of racing clouds, sunshine, and the giggle of his daughter coming from beside him.

It's all gone in a matter of seconds before he hits the ground. He nearly clips his head on a counter on the way down, but by some sheer force of luck, avoids it. He collapses on the floor with all the grace of a middle-aged father: hard and with the understanding that he won't be getting up on his own anytime soon.

He's hefted onto his feet by the two remaining creatures, both of whom take an arm each and drag him out of the kitchen. With his thigh still screaming at him, Hugh can barely get his own feet to work, and panic has ensnared him fully like a rabbit in a trap.

How the hell is he going to get out of this? How much longer until that pain from the spell subsides...if it subsides? He isn't sure now. He's pushed himself by performing that second spell. His body feels as if it's just survived being microwaved.

Out of the cafeteria, the clanking, chattering monsters haul him up the stairs toward the second floor.

"You're gonna looooove it here," one of them spoke, her jaw hanging crookedly as she finished her sentence. He watched a string of black-tinged drool drop from the corner of her mouth and land on his arm.

"Youuu can be whoever you want heeeeere," the other adds.

They just won't stop talking. Fucking chatterboxes the both of them.

They pull him down the hall upstairs toward that last room and his stomach turns as he hears screams coming from the open door. The Mark. Was it already too late? Have they begun tearing into him like a deranged mechanic into an old car?

He thinks briefly on the Mechanic whose body he'd left in that garage out in the middle of the desert and wipes it away. Where is Amos when he needs him? Usually, his voice is impossible to get rid of, the memory of it burrowing into him like some sort of insect. Reminding him of the past. But it also keeps him on track, too, and that is something he needs right now. Something to help him ignore the fiery pain in his leg and focus.

But he doesn't appear.

They go through the door.

Hugh's heart thrashes with the sight of the horrible room. The chatterbox that grabbed the Mark is holding him down while another straps him into the table. A few more of them stand along the far wall, staring into space like the undead.

When the Mark sees him, he drops his head back against the stretcher and groans. "Fuck me. Is this how we die? Is this it?"

Hugh doesn't answer though he's not convinced this isn't how they die.

"Ah!" A figure appears from the back corner of the room, shielded by doctor's scrubs and a blue helmet with a plastic face shield. The face behind it is familiar. Several more wrinkles, his hair greyed, the round wire-framed glasses exactly the same. Mr. Park.

He smiles. "We don't get a lot of people sneaking in here trying to disrupt our therapy sessions, but when we do it's because they desperately need help. Whether they realize it or not. I mean, who doesn't in this day and age, am I right?"

"Where's my sister?" the Mark demands through his teeth. "Where is she?"

Park frowns. "Take a look around, kiddo." He waves at the standing audience of chatterboxes. "Everyone is here."

Terror seeps into the Mark's face. His eyes bounce between the various faces watching him, back and forth, back and forth until...he focuses. Hugh can't quite make out who he sees in the near darkness, but when the sob breaks in the Mark's throat, he knows it's too late.

"Ruby?" His voice is flat. "No..."

One of the chatterboxes' heads perks up, a slow recognition. She steps away from the others stiffly, meandering a little in tiny steps like a doll until the operatory light casts her in its glow.

*Christ.*

Hugh wants to look away but finds himself unable, the sheer horror locking his eyes on her. Her hair is pulled back in a disheveled ponytail, her once blue eyes sunken and glassy. The hardware holding her mouth together is more pronounced than some of her fellow patients, wingnuts fastening bolts through the ruined skin of her cheeks. When her jaw opens, it's with a sound akin to a can opener. "Dy...lan?"

The Mark's face is twisted, the shock quickly doused by fury as he bucks against the straps. "I'm gonna kill you!" he screams at Park. "I'm gonna fucking kill you!"

A MOMENT.

It strikes Hugh like the hour hand of a clock completing its slow revolution from one number to another. Amos reached across their bed to clasp his hand. His fingers were warm, his smile cunning. Everything inside of Hugh glowed when he thought about their life. How it used to be.

How they would walk on the windiest days just to say they got some extra air. How they'd go to the grocery store with a list and always end up adding another bottle of wine or an extra bar of chocolate. How Amos hummed Fleetwood Mac's "Say You Love Me" while he brushed his teeth every morning. How they always made pancakes on Sundays for Ella. How they never allowed themselves to go to bed angry with one another.

Gone. All gone.

HIS GRAY FACE.

His gray eyes stared at some odd corner of the ceiling.

A dribble of vomit like oatmeal had dried on the corner of his mouth and spilled on the pillow.

All sound receded. In the din of a growing ring in Hugh's ears, his heartbeat boomed inside it like a drum in a cavern.

He hadn't been there.

He wasn't there when Amos needed him.

His husband had died alone in this strange green room with no one to hold his hand or kiss his forehead or tell him...

Hugh pinched the bridge of his nose and looked out at the sunshine, at the field of flowers out the window. He hadn't seen anyone when he'd arrived. No nurses. No orderlies or doctors. Just the patients still in their beds, every one of them dead.

He didn't remember going downstairs. One moment he was looking outside, the next: shouting. The doctor's office door was open, Doctor Mann himself sitting on the ground with a half empty bottle of whiskey next to him.

Hugh's fingers clutched at the starched fabric of a white overcoat. He couldn't see; tears blurred his gaze. "I'll kill you!" he shouted, yanking Doctor Mann up from his stupor. "What the fuck is wrong with you? How could you—"

"—KILL YOU, YOU SON OF A BITCH!"

Park rolls his eyes. "That's what they all say." He walks toward the table where the Mark is strapped and puts a hand on Ruby's shoulder. "She was in a lot of pain. A *lot* of pain. We really needed to get all of it out. And what's better than talking, right? Talking always helps."

"Talking, talking, talking," the chatterboxes echoed, though not in uniformity, like a deranged recitation of "Row, Row, Row Your Boat" gone out of hand.

"She talked a lot about you. About *your* pain. How she wished you could share it and talk about it together as brother and sister." Mr. Park picked up a tool from the tray. "I've never done a pair before. Siblings. It feels like this is meant to be."

Before the Mark can protest, one of the chatterboxes gags him with a spare leather strap.

Ruby leans over him. "It's gonna be great, Dylan. We're going to talk sooo much."

Hugh's breath trembles as he recognizes Amos now standing amidst the chatterboxes against the opposite wall.

"Sharing our troubles is the key to smooooth sailing from now on." She smiles and the gears in her cheeks click. "Smooth like—"

"I'LL KILL YOU! What the fuck is wrong with you? How could you—"

"I didn't," Doctor Mann sobbed.

He was so superficial now. Hugh didn't understand how he didn't notice it before. The immaculate act completely made up for their benefit. As though he'd only played doctor. The golden rings and watches and leather shoes and expensive suits and perfectly trimmed hair and perfectly cut nails...

Mann blubbered. Mann drank.

"Steele did it."

"He did this."

"I would never do this."

Hugh felt abysmally small. How else would this hospice center in the middle of nowhere get the money it needed? It couldn't have been from the family of his patients, not completely.

Steele.

Hugh bristled and deflated. And put his fist through a wall.

"WE NEED TO BURY THEM."
Mann looked up at him in confusion.
Hugh simply repeated the words.

THE TWO MEN spent the rest of the day digging graves. Until the sun swiveled and dipped into the mountains in the distance. Until the stars glistened in the purple dark.

It's the hardest thing he'd ever done. Even building their back porch, laying out their garden, planting trees, landscaping... Moving that piano into the living room for him to practice on...

Nothing so heavy as carrying the bodies of the dead one by one down to these too shallow holes, wrapping them in sheets. Amos was the lightest and filled him with the most sorrow.

He couldn't bring himself to say anything, not even a goodbye as he placed his husband in the hole and started covering him in dirt.

THE DOCTOR is still speaking. The Mark howls through the leather strap. The chatterboxes look on, the first time he's heard them so silent.

The throbbing in Hugh's leg is nothing more than a tingle.

"And what about me?" he finally calls to the Doctor.

Park whirls around to look at him; his spectacles have dropped to the end of his nose. "Oh. Yes." He steps away from the stretcher and approaches him. "You. You can wait your turn just like all these fine people have before y—" He's close enough now to recognize Hugh.

To remember him.

IT WAS IN A MOMENT OF WEAKNESS that Hugh found himself dialing the number on the card. Who else did he have to turn to? The world was falling into ruin. Ella was inconsolable. His neighbor's house was foreclosed upon. Town was hazardous: looting, violence in the streets, censuring, silencing...

He'd sold the house.

He'd sold his car.

All to pay for Amos's treatment.

And now Amos is gone.

If the Park's clinic would house he and Ella, help them both... Maybe there was a way they could get back on their feet.

Hugh was able to find someone who would give them a ride to the office where Doctor Park's clinic was kept: a squat brick office building on a hill surrounded by other office buildings, all of which seemed empty. In the twilight, moths fluttered around the streetlamp outside. The only sound was its obnoxious buzz.

The receptionist at the front desk eyed them disapprovingly as they waited. Hugh couldn't imagine how awful they must have smell. It had been almost two weeks without a shower or a bath. The electricity had shut off when the power grid went down. Ella had knots in her hair he couldn't get out.

Park's office was spartan. Only a few books on the shelves, the whitest rug Hugh had ever seen, crimson-colored walls and a singular window that looked out over the violet sky.

"You weren't interested in talking last time we met," Park frowned. "What changed?"

Hugh opened his mouth and his voice dried up. He'd lost everything. But he couldn't...he just *couldn't* speak. Speaking it out loud felt like a different kind of defeat, another level. He was asking for help and he didn't want it. He didn't want anyone getting near him, anyone who could threaten Ella. He didn't want to give anyone the chance to shatter whatever was left of their family.

Park cocked his head. "Nothing clearly."

They were back on the street in less than fifteen minutes.

A bird's call echoed across the sky. Ella hugged her coat closer to herself. "I'm hungry," she moaned.

And Hugh felt utterly alone for the first time in his life.

HUGH WAITS FOR THE SHOCK to hit in Park's eyes. The slight widening of his pupils, perhaps a lip dropping. Something to indicate that he remembers the day where he turned Hugh and his daughter away to the cold. Something to show that he was a monster before he even began making real monsters...

But it doesn't come.

"Were they your kids?" Park asks instead. "How heartwarming. A whole family to convert. A whole unit that can now say all they need to say to one another without the fear and anxiety that comes along with it. And we'll all exist harmoniously here on the edge of oblivion..." He's singing to himself, humming a song that it takes Hugh a moment to recognize and when he does, he feels the heat rise in his belly: "What A Wonderful World".

Park picks up a scalpel from the blood and oil-splattered tray next to the Mark and lets it glisten in the light for a moment before he leans in.

The Mark's screams bounce off the ceiling.

"You're going to look for me everywhere you go and you're always going to see me," Amos had told him days before he died. "Don't be afraid to admit to yourself that I'm actually gone."

Hugh blinks. Fresh tears have sparked in the corners of his eyes.

Damn it.

God *damn* it.

The echo from Amos's words emanates through the air from where he stands amongst the broken people, the chatterboxes.

And beneath it, anger floods through him. Like saturating sponge cake, every pore of him is infused by the rage, by the loss, by the goddamn emptiness. He realizes in this opening abyss within him that all his pain has fled and now all that remains is what is left. Who he is. The parts of Amos he's held onto. What being with Amos transformed him into. The remains.

Hugh says words that he hasn't uttered before, words that he never said. Words Amos fed him when he was in need:

"Don't be afraid."

The energy lances through his body, coiling in his blood and galvanizing him.

Park trembles, his core vibrating as though someone is charging him with a defibrillator. His tongue swells and nearly eclipses the oh-shape of his mouth, his eyes rolling back and fingers spasming. The drill revs and drops to the floor, nearly putting a hole in the doctor's own shoe.

Hugh focuses, snares every tendril of darkness, every morsel of loneliness that's made a home inside of him for the last several years and lets it glide along the current of sorcery from his hand to Park's body.

It doesn't belong inside of him anymore.

release.
it's
exhilarating.
like flying.
every darkness
every cascading wave
or thought
of pain
of love
of death
is flowing
from him
away

and...

...JUST LIKE THAT, IT'S OVER.

Whatever quivering, hissing mass is left of Park's body crumples to the floor like a heap of butchered meat. The Mark's screams echo through the room. The Chatterboxes are crying. They're holding their heads and wailing, their mechanical sobs like shattered xylophones.

All of that release is followed by numbness. It sweeps through Hugh almost like a strong gust of wind heralding a coming storm. For a few seconds, he isn't sure what to do. He isn't sure he's all in one piece. His skin tingles, buzzing with the latent energy from the spell, his brain swirling on the cotton candy sweetness of Amos's everlasting words and as it fades...

He moves into action.

He crosses the room, shoving the mewling Ruby out of the way and unbuckles the Mark from the stretcher.

The kid leaps off and cowers for a moment to himself, hands brushing over his skin. When his gaze drops on that of his sister, he rushes to her side.

"Ruby, it's okay. I'm going to get you help. I'm going to get you—"

But the girl isn't moving.

None of the chatterboxes are moving.

They've all gone still, like someone has flipped their switches. Fallen across the floor like toddlers at the end of their tantrums, limbs entangled and mouths open in silent screams.

There's not a breath among them.

The Mark touches her skin and flinches. "She's cold."

Hugh swallows. "She's been dead for some time."

"How..." The Mark's eyes quickly flash to anger. "How did this happen?"

Hugh doesn't answer. When he approaches Park's body, he pushes up the sleeve of the doctor's scrubs to see a collection of tattoos, of scratches, of carved runes that stretch up past his elbow. Hugh suspects they probably cover his whole body for the elaborateness of the spell. A blend of mechanical engineering and sorcery...

He puts his hand on the Mark's shoulder. "I'll explain once we're out of here." He starts for the door but the Mark remains where he is. Hugh hears the faintest sniffle.

"She trusted me. I was supposed to look after her. So, I can't just...leave her like this. We've got to..."

"Bury her?" Hugh answers.

"I don't want to leave her here. Not here."

There isn't soft dirt for miles. They're in the heart of Mal Verdugo. In a sandstorm. In the night.

But Hugh nods.

The Mark hefts his sister into his arms in a fireman's carry and they find their way down to the ground floor.

# ACCEPTANCE

# MAL VERDUGO

THERE IS A MOUNTAIN on a road between Mal Verdugo and the small town of Pria where flowers bloom in spite of no rain. The phenomenon has brought people from near and far on a pilgrimage. Several see the flowers as a symbol of something beyond themselves, a higher power, a miracle. For others, it's about beauty, something that dies every day since the Collapse.

The Mark requests to bring his sister here and Hugh does so without a word. He waits in the car as the boy carries her into the sea of pink and yellow blossoms, passing the occasional parishioner in their dingy clothes, with their covered faces.

"*What will you do?*" Amos asks him as the Mark disappears from sight.

"What I can," Hugh mutters.

"*You're not going to kill him?*"

Hugh stares into the flowers.

"Well?"

Steele is sitting this time. Hugh doesn't think he's seen Steele sit in years, not since the first time they sat across from one another in that hotel back in his home town: the Hierophant Hotel. Not since he was first offered the job that he refused.

The job that got Amos killed.

Hugh's photos of the brother and sister are almost artistic. Others he'd taken had been scattershot, blurry, meant to hide the truth or at least lessen its horribleness on his own psyche. And they had screamed of subterfuge. So, he took his time with these. Because surely, Steele would see the intention in them if he did. He'd understand the pain inflicted.

"Damn," Steele mutters as he flicks through each one with a thumb on his phone. "If I didn't know any better, I'd think you're beginning to like this stuff, Maestro."

Hugh doesn't speak. He doesn't need to.

"I've seen this work before," Steele says. "Some doctor fellow I lent some money to some years back. Real wackadoodle. Don't suppose you came across him, did you?"

Because who would have the money for Park's clinic and all the advertising that had come with it? Who had the money to sweep his accusations under the rug?

Steele.

That's who.

Hugh answers. "I did. I turned him into a steaming pile of meat. Last picture."

Steele flips to it and his mouth forms a straight line. "Leaping lizards, that's disgusting." He stands up and plops the phone on the desk. "Guess I'll cross him off the list. He was a ways down but that's okay—I applaud the creative dispatch method. Now, who's next?"

Pancakes.

Coffee.

The hiss of the coffee pots, the sizzle of bacon hitting a griddle.

Hugh sips from his mug.

The Mark stares down at his. "So, this is the part where you tell me you've spiked my coffee right?" He glances up at Hugh. "Because he wasn't convinced. Steele?"

"He bought it. Those Chatterboxes were so mangled, he couldn't tell the difference. In his mind, you're just one of the many bodies still out there."

"Why save me?" The Mark's lip twisted a little. "I don't get it. You could have taken me out at any moment. I'm no one special."

"Because..." Hugh carved a wedge out of his pancake with a fork and speared it. "You reminded me of someone I used to be."

"But you're not anymore?" His eyes widen. "I mean... I'm sorry. That wasn't very fair."

"Not anymore." Hugh bites the pancake from the fork and slowly chews. "Perhaps someday I can be again."

Another few moments pass in silence. Hugh eats more of his pancakes.

The Mark goes to cut into his and stops with his knife part of the way. "I can't stop thinking about her. I can't stop thinking about what you told me: that Steele gave Park that money. He's the reason she's gone. He's the reason I got in debt in the first place."

Hugh nods. "Steele is omnipresent. He has fingers everywhere."

"How does evil like that continue to spread?" The Mark holds his knife in a death grip. "How can so many people just stand by and watch someone like that destroy everyone around them? How is that allowed?"

"You're young." Hugh holds the coffee mug between his hands, letting the heat radiate into his fingers. "Evil will always be there, shrinking and swelling. But it's indifference that's the killer. Indifference has killed millions. Indifference caused the economic collapse. Indifference banished everyone to this godforsaken drought-fucked land."

"So why the hell haven't we done something about it?"

"Because fear is a strong motivator. Because everyone is scared." Hugh clears his throat. "Even me."

The Mark slumps in his seat, curling his hand around the cup of orange drink concentrate on the table. His lip judders. "I can't... I can't stop hearing Ruby's voice. Every time I sleep, I hear her calling for me and I can't do anything..."

Hugh frowned. "You're going to look for her everywhere you go and you're going to see her...hear her. But you can't be afraid to admit to yourself that she's gone."

The Mark folds his arms into a nest on the table and cries.

After a few moments, Hugh reaches a hand across and sets it on one of the Mark's.

The kid looks up at him, his eyes red, and sniffles. "I want to take him down. Steele. There has to be a way."

For the first time in what feels like forever, hope flutters up from the darkness within Hugh's mind. "Yes, well... Someday. Someday, when the moment is right. Until then, we stay alive. Staying alive is fighting. Not succumbing is fighting." He gives the Mark's hand a squeeze. "So, let's fight."

# MONTHS AGO

"Y OU WANT ME TO…WHAT?"

The Guide was, no doubt, confused. Every moment they spent out on the street, the cold of night leeched from Hugh's sanity. The lullaby of the griddle called to him, the fake maple syrup aroma, the coffee…

"Take them." He nodded to the car. "I'm sure there's something in there that'll be useful to you and your…customers."

The pink radiance from the Garden of Delight's neon light bathed them and the sidewalk, the only thing still glowing at this ungodly hour of the morning. It was the only place Hugh knew of where he could bring them.

The Guide furrowed her dark brows before looking into the open back door of the car. "How many plants are in there?"

"A dozen or so."

The green leaves covered almost every square inch of his backseat, of the legroom space and the rear deck. They'd be at home in the place for people who floated their miseries away with the help of herbal cocktails, powerful stimulants, and mesmerizing hallucinogens.

Something skittered over the woman's face. "My boss might not like it."

Hugh's eyes followed the building with its crisp, clean edges all the way to the top floor, to the light that he knew was hidden behind dimmed glass. "Will he even notice?"

When she didn't answer, he returned his gaze to her. Fear, a kind he knew too well was mirrored in her eyes. And something else. Daring. "Most likely. But…" She leaned in, wrapped her skinny arms around the pot for the monstera and heaved it out. "He'll get over it."

She could get in serious trouble for this, he knew. The Guide was merely that; an attendant for the people who came here to get their fix. She was there to make sure they didn't overdose, they didn't hallucinate and kill one another, that they didn't wander out into traffic and kill themselves…

Her boss stowed himself in a room at the top much like his own did. Hugh had seen him once at the Pancake House stuffing a Southwestern omelet and hashbrowns down his gullet like a pelican. He was messy, didn't like small talk with the waitresses, and ordered them around as if they were his own personal staff.

But this Guide wasn't afraid of him enough to say no.

The idea of smiling at her rebelliousness alit in his mind. Instead, he nodded and helped bring each plant inside to its new home.

Amos's hand trembled in his. Hugh had never seen him like this in his life. Even when Amos was sick, be it with a cold or a stomach bug, he never seemed to lose his spark, his wit, his quickness.

But as they sat in the little dining room of the hospice center over their cold bowls of cheddar broccoli soup, it dawned on Hugh how much of a shadow Amos had become of his former self. And that was when the fear slipped inside and nestled close. There was no more pretending. There was no more wishing for the best.

He was going to lose Amos. He was going to lose everything that made him who he was before he took his final breath.

He'd be alone.

Truly alone.

But Amos smiled at him and said, "It's a beautiful day, huh?"

And he turned to look outside. To the flowers. To the sounds of the peepers in the grass. To the sun turning its afternoon golden orange.

It was. In spite of it all, it was.

# ACKNOWLEDGEMENTS

VULPINE CURSE feels like the most personal book I've written so far within the Deadlands series. We are four months into the regime of a president who is trying to force our country back into its most rudimentary era. Trying to erase all of the endeavors made along the way to make it a fairer and safer place for everyone. To highlight diversity and showcase how those diversities make us a stronger country.

Every day under this horrible government brings a new more terrible news story and every day, it feels like a chore to get up and go to work. To keep doing the same routine as always just to survive. To shackle the growing dread and fear and grief away and put on a smile.

But writing horror is my way of standing up. Writing something feral, something that knocks back against these awful and archaic attempts to stamp our country into a cookie-cutter from almost a hundred years ago... That's where my power is.

So, I will go on writing them. I will go on writing about LGBTQIA+ experiences, highlighting our voices, doing my part as a member of that community to make sure we are not erased.

We will not vanish.

We will survive. We will not succumb. We will fight.

photo by Colin Borowske © 2025

Katherine Silva is an ace Maine horror author, a connoisseur of coffee, and victim of cat shenanigans. Her favorite flavors of the genre mix grief and existentialism which she combines with her love of the New England wilderness in her works. She is a three-time Maine Literary Award finalist for speculative fiction. Katherine is also editor-in-chief of Strange Wilds Press. You can find out all about her work at katherinesilvaauthor.com.